crawford cowboys

Books 1-3

kat baxter

Crawford Cowboys

Kat Baxter

Copyright 2022 by Kat Baxter

This novel is a work of fiction. Names, characters, places and incidents are either the product of the author's imagination or have been used fictitiously and are not to be construed as real. Any resemblance to persons, living or dead, actual events, locales or organizations is entirely coincidental.

All Rights Reserved.

No part of this book may be reproduced or transmitted in any form, or by any electronic or mechanical means, including photocopying, recording, or by an information storage and retrieval system, without the express written permission of the author or publisher, except where permitted by law.

Edited by: Emily Beierle-McKaskle

Copyeditor: Jenny Steward

Book cover: Cover Girl Designs

With regard to digital publication, be advised that any alteration of font size or spacing by the reader could change the author's original format.

❦ Created with Vellum

lone star ex-con

. . .

Callie

I know "Roe" is different the minute he steps into

the library. It's not his scowl or his tattoos or even the intelligence he tries so hard to hide. There's something in his eyes that calls to me. I feel a connection with him I can't explain. Of course he's also the most devastatingly handsome man I've ever laid eyes on. He needs a wife. And he can provide something I want. So despite the fact that he's way hotter than me, I offer to meet him at the altar. But I never expected to fall in love with my husband.

Monroe

I just got out of prison. I literally have blood on my hands. It doesn't matter if it was an accident or even justified. I'm tainted. One look at the bespectacled, curvy librarian, and I'm hooked. Clean, educated, and polished, Callie is beautiful, sweet, and the sheriff's sister. She's the last person I should want because I'm the worst person for her. But when she offers to marry me to meet the conditions of my grandfather's will, I practically run to the courthouse.

one

. . .

Lone Star

Monroe

I'm in the library on my day off, trying to upload a week's worth of work for my online class and trying not to notice the skirt the hot red-haired librarian is wearing today when the first text comes in. I know it's from someone in the family because it's the custom ringtone Madison created for us. I ignore the text because I have to get this paper turned in for my Auditing Theory and Practices class today and the internet out at the ranch is slow as fuck.

Another text rolls in. I glance down at my phone and see my brother's name before I slip my phone into silent mode. I live in the same house as three of my brothers. I saw Quinn six hours ago. Therefore, there is nothing he needs to tell me that tops finishing this paper. Besides, I have enough distractions already.

And by distractions, I mean the sexy librarian.

The red hair. The curls. The infuriating buttons on her cardigan sweaters. There is nothing overtly sexy about the way this woman dresses, but, despite that, everything about her does it for me.

I get one day off a week from the ranch when I can cram in all the work for my online classes. Thursday. Storytime day at the library. Which means the sexy librarian is always around on Thursdays.

My brothers and sister and I own and work a ranch just outside the tiny town of Saddle Creek, Texas. Since cattle don't give a shit about weekends, it's a job that requires long days, and staggered days off. I could ask my brothers to change days, but there would be questions. Questions I don't have answers for.

What am I going to say? I need to change my day off because there's a woman in the library I imagine fucking eight ways to Sunday every time I see her? No way in hell am I admitting that to my brothers.

So I come here every Thursday to download all my work for the coming week, upload all the work I've done, and quietly lose my mind imagining what it would be like to unbutton one of her sweaters. One tiny button at a time.

By eleven, the kids and harried parents are starting to fill up the nook in the children's section.

It's a steady stream of kids trotting past the front desk and calling, "Hello, Ms. Burton!"

I have the perfect view of her from my computer. She greets each kid by name, beaming at them like their presence at storytime made her day. That smile unlocks something inside me. I'm not even sure what it is. All I know is, the more I see it, the more I crave it. Only, I want it aimed at me.

Today she's wearing a blue plaid skirt, a simple white button-up blouse and a navy blue cardigan buttoned halfway up. All those fucking buttons. She's like a goddamn present I want to unwrap every single day.

By the time she starts reading aloud, some book about a pet pig, I'm hard enough to embarrass myself. Thankfully the kids are hidden by the half stacks of books in the children's section, because it's bad enough getting a half chub in the public library, let alone surrounded by kids. But Callie Burton turns me the fuck on. I force myself to focus on my school work to distract my mind because now is not the time to be fantasizing about my sexy librarian and her many buttons.

Between the distraction of her reading out loud and the constant vibrating of my phone on the desk beside me, it takes forever for me to finish the paper, run it through the grammar software, and send it off to my online professor.

I log out of the library computer just as the last of

the kids are leaving. Storytime is long over and Ms. Burton is checking out books for them. I walk past the main desk on my way out. I know what I should do. I need to keep my head down and walk out without even glancing at her.

Because a woman like Ms. Burton ... a good woman, smart, educated, and kind, in addition to being exactly the kind of sexy that drives me crazy ... a woman like that is way out of my league.

I know what I should do, but I've never been the kind of guy who is good at following orders, even when they're orders I give myself. So instead of doing the right thing, I slow my steps as I approach the desk. I wait for her to look up and meet my gaze. Her cheeks tinge pink before I say a word.

"Ms. Burton," I say slowly, tipping my head in a nod.

Her eyes go wide and her pupils dilate. The pink in her cheeks darkens and spreads down her neck, disappearing beneath the buttoned up collar of her white shirt. After a second, she presses her lips together in disapproval and turns her attention back to the kid, handing over a stack of books.

I'm about to step up to the counter and ask her for a book recommendation when my phone rings. Only two people in my contact list will ring through when I've silenced notification: Quinn and Madison. Quinn hates talking on the phone, so I know it must be Madison. She's the only girl in the family.

I duck my head and turn to the library door as I pull my phone out of my back pocket. Hitching my backpack up on my shoulder, I push through the double doors and out on to the street as I accept the call.

"Hey, Mad, what's up?"

It's cool for March, but the sky is clear and so bright it almost hurts to look at it after being inside all morning.

"What's up is you need to fucking check your texts." Madison sounds out of breath like she's walking somewhere, and way more annoyed than she usually does when she's talking to me. She has sass for days, but I'm her favorite, so she usually reins it in around me. "Where the hell have you been?"

"At the library. Why?"

"The library?" She snorts. "That's where you spend your day off?"

"Yeah. I spend my day off at the library. Anything to get out of the damn house." Quinn, Harrison and I all live at the ranch in the house we grew up in. Hayes, Harrison's twin, lives in Austin, a couple of hundred miles east of Saddle Creek and Johnny is still off at Texas A&M. I don't know what the hell we're going to do when he graduates in May and moves home, because with the three of us in the house it's already too much. "The library is quiet and the internet doesn't suck. So yeah, that's where I go."

"Okay, nerd," she teases. "Just get your ass over to Ace's."

My steps slow as I approach the beat up old truck I've been driving since high school. "Ace's? What?"

"Emergency family meeting. Just get here." A door squeaks in the background and the sounds of passing cars are replaced by low chatter and the clinking of dishes. "And read your damn texts."

She hangs up before I can say anything else.

I open my truck long enough to throw my bag on the floorboard, then shut the door and lock it. The library is only a block off the town square and since I'm parked in public parking, I leave my truck where it is and head back toward the square, where Ace's, a local burger joint that's been a landmark forever, is located.

I pull up my texts. I have over a dozen texts in The Jolly Ranchers text chain. That's what Madison named the family text chain. Because she thinks she's funny like that.

<The Jolly Ranchers>

> ***Quinn:*** *Just left the Rocking C. We need to meet up ASAP.*
> ***Harrison:*** *What's up? The Dark Lord pissing you off again? What'd he do this time?*

Madison: You can't let him bait you. If you get pissed off every time he calls you a pussy, it just amuses him. Don't let him get to you.

Quinn: Just get the troops together. Preferably somewhere with drinks. I'll be there in three hours.

Johnny: Drinks? We're meeting for drinks? I'll be there.

Hayes: I'm at work. In Austin, remember? I can't just leave and meet y'all for drinks.

Harrison: If Quinn says it's an emergency, then it's an emergency.

Madison: In other words, get your ass home pretty boy.

Madison: Johnny, you stay where you are. You have midterms next week.

Quinn: No, we need Johnny too.

Harrison: Hayes, can you wait until Johnny gets to Austin so he can ride with you?

Hayes: No, because I'm not fucking leaving work for this drama. Whatever it is, y'all handle it without me.

Johnny: I can drive myself.

Harrison: Just got off the phone with Quinn. He's not fucking around. Get your ass to Ace's by 1:00

> ***Johnny***: *Wait. Can Monroe even go into Ace's?*
>
> ***Madison***: *Yes, dumbass. He can go into Ace's. It's a restaurant that serves alcohol, not a bar. His parole is specifically about bars.*
>
> ***Johnny***: *Just asking*
>
> ***Johnny***: *<GIF of a person shrugging>*
>
> ***Madison***: *Stop texting while you drive.*

The texts keep going but I stop reading and pick up the pace because it's already after one-thirty.

I walk into Ace's and nostalgia stabs me like a knife to the chest.

Inside Ace's, the lighting is dim and the air is filled with the smell of beer, grease, and smoke. Of course, no one has smoked in Ace's in probably twenty years, but I can still smell the smoke that seeped into the wood paneling from all those decades that it was a bar before the current owner took over and made it into a restaurant.

It feels like a Texas honky-tonk, which is probably why it regularly makes whatever best-fill-in-the-blank-in-Texas list that Texas Monthly is peddling. Best chicken fried steak. Best burger. Best fries. Best arugula salad topped with locally-sourced artisanal goat cheese. Whatever. Whatever foods trendy people care about, they serve it here, along with a hefty serving of Texas flavor.

I haven't stepped foot into Ace's in years. Not since I got out the Army—because I hadn't really had the chance yet back then. And not since I got out of prison—because even though it's not a bar, it's too close to being a bar for my comfort.

Still, Quinn called the emergency family meeting here. Despite the string of texts, I still don't know what the hell the meeting is about. But Quinn isn't a drama queen. If he's called us all together, we show up.

Plus, Ace's does have good fries, so the afternoon won't be a total loss.

I find the rest of the Crawfords sitting around a table in the back corner of the restaurant. True to his threats, Hayes is nowhere to be seen—which isn't a huge surprise—but Quinn, Harrison, Madison, and Johnny are all there. Each of them has a pint in front of them. Madison's is fresh. The guys' are almost empty. They are all wearing expressions ranging from shocked to grim.

I slide into one of the empty chairs. "Who pissed in your coffee this morning?"

Madison pauses mid-sip and glares at me.

There's a fair amount of maternal chiding in that look. Out of all of us, Madison looks the most like mom and I see the resemblance strongest when she's giving me a look that says *Sit down. Shut up. And mind your manners.*

Before I can ask what the hell is going on, a waitress I don't recognize ambles over and deposits another round of pints in front of my brothers. She cocks a hip and smiles in my direction. "You want a Shiner, too?"

"Just water. Thanks."

Shiner Bock, the best beer in Texas, is brewed not that far from here, but, like Ace's fries, it's another thing I've gone without. When you're out on parole, you don't drink unless you want to end up back in prison. Even though I've never had a drinking problem, I still don't want to risk it.

A moment later, there's a water in front of me. No one has said anything and I can tell from the set of Quinn's jaw that he was waiting for the waitress to put some distance between her ears and his words. Like any small town, gossip in Saddle Creek is as popular as a Church potluck.

"What the hell is up?" I ask, scooting my chair closer.

Quinn clenches his jaw like he's too upset to talk and it's Madison who answers.

"Grandpa Crawford had a stroke."

I raise an eyebrow. "*Grandpa* Crawford?" I ask, because none of us call him that. Then I lean across the table to clink my water glass against her pint. "If

Voldemort's finally ready to kick the bucket, why the hell aren't these celebration drinks?"

I don't want to sound like an insensitive ass, but our grandfather is mean, controlling, and manipulative. Thus the nickname.

Finally, Quinn answers. "He had the stroke nine days ago."

"And we just now found out about it?"

Quinn, normally not much a drinker, downs most of the pint before setting it down, his expression grim. "Lewis didn't want us to know."

"That fucker," Harrison mutters.

Lewis, our dad's younger brother, is absolutely a dick. Where our grandfather, who we openly call The Dark Lord, is pure, self-serving evil, with a heavy dose of racism and classism thrown on top, Uncle Lewis is a more subtle form of evil. He's conniving and manipulative, the kind of guy who will butter you up, grin, slap you on the shoulder, and then shiv you in the side before you have a chance to see the knife. Metaphorically speaking. So keeping with our Harry Potter theme, we started calling him Uncle Umbridge.

"I don't get it," I admit. "He just wasn't going to tell us? How was that going to work?"

Quinn shakes his head. "We're here in Saddle Creek. The big ranch is nearly three hundred miles away. There's no way we would know anything is up unless someone contacts us. The only reason I went up to the big ranch at all is because Aiden texted me yesterday and hinted that I should visit."

Madison says, gently, "It doesn't look good."

I'm still trying to wrap my head around the idea that our grandfather, The Dark Lord himself, had a stroke. I would have sworn the asshole was too stubborn to be ill and too mean to die.

"The question you should all be asking" –Quinn tips his glass in my direction—"is why Uncle Umbridge didn't want us to know about the stroke." Quinn sighs heavily. I'm just gonna cut to the chase because there's a lot of legal crap that frankly I'm going to have to have Blake explain to me like I'm a damn child. But the gist of it is, that we all need to get married."

"Wait, what?" Johnny asks. "I'm barely twenty-two. I have wild oats and such."

Madison ruffles his blond hair. "Adorable, but no one wants to hear about your oats so just keep them in your pants, will you?"

From the corner of my eye, I see the normally unflappable Harrison shift in his chair.

"We need pre-nups and quick marriages so that when dear old Voldemort finally dies, we actually get to keep our family ranch and it doesn't get tied up in legal crap with his trust that gets eventually turned over to Uncle Umbridge," Quinn says.

"This doesn't make any sense," Madison says.

"Logistically, no, it doesn't," Quinn says. "But

legally, he has the right to do all of this because unfortunately everything is in his name, not ours."

Quinn quickly fills us in on how the trust is set up and what it means. Most of it is Greek to me, but I know enough to understand that he's right. Voldermort set it up so we lose it all if we're not married by the time he dies. We have to get married now.

"I'm a convicted felon," I say. "Who the hell is going to marry me?"

"Listen, I know this is a lot to dump on all of you, but just do what you can. We can meet up again this weekend and try to brainstorm ideas. Anyone dating anyone?" Quinn asks.

"Hayes probably is," Harrison says.

"Yeah, but it's illegal to marry more than one woman at a time," Johnny says with a snort.

But I'm still lost in thought thinking about the fact that I have nothing to offer any woman. A certain sexy redheaded librarian flashes through my mind, but of all the women in Saddle Creek, she especially could find a man better than me.

two

· · ·

Callie

Spring break at the public library is both great and terrible. Great because I love having the library flooded with kids. The week is full of daily special events—puppet shows, magic shows, and face painting. Terrible because of the long days and the pure, unfiltered chaos.

Today's event will likely be the highlight though, with the petting zoo brought to us by The Farm Lady, aka my best friend Rory.

This is the fifth year in a row Rory has brought her collection of miniature horses, tiny goats, and fluffy rabbits. Rory and I met when she first moved to Saddle Creek six years ago. She grew up in the hustle and bustle of Dallas, but she is happiest surrounded by barnyard animals and compost.

She is currently outside setting up all her temporary pens in the grassy park outside the library. I'm busy handing out flyers for our summer reading program to all the parents when my part-time employee, Veronica sidles up.

"He's here again," Veronica says from between her teeth.

I am well aware which *he* she means, but I don't know why she's telling me. Monroe Crawford has been a frequent visitor to the library for the last several weeks. He's a quiet and polite man, but those qualities are only noticeable after you get over the shock of his appearance. Well over six feet tall and broad and muscular, he looks more like a professional football player than a man who haunts the stacks of a small town public library. Yet here he is, not quite daily, but multiple times a week.

"I'm sure he'll come speak to you soon," I tell Veronica.

She snorts. "He's not here to see me."

I turn to stare at the college-age woman. Veronica is blonde, young, and gorgeous. I'm sure she's the reason he comes here so often. Since she's clearly being modest, I say, "Well, I suppose he could just be that voracious of a reader."

She rolls her eyes. "Callie, please tell you're not

that blind. That man watches you like a mouse hunting a bird."

My heart thumps. "I beg your pardon? He does no such thing. Also, you have that wrong because mice don't hunt birds. Do you mean a cat?"

Veronica shakes her head, smiling smugly. "You'll see."

I click my tongue at her. "You are ridiculous. And also, this is proof that you're a romantic at heart and clearly belong in our romance book club. We meet this Friday night. You should join us."

"I might." She leaves behind the counter with the rolling cart of books. "I've got to go shelve these."

I nod. "When you're done, please print more flyers about the summer reading program and just set them on the counter. Peter will be back soon to run circulation while I'm outside with the kids and the animals."

I watch Veronica round the stacks, shaking my head at her overly vivid imagination. Despite that, my eyes find Mr. Crawford sitting at the computer he normally chooses. I nearly jump out of my skin when I realize he's looking directly at me. Veronica's words still fresh in my mind, I give him a smile that feels tight and unnatural, before turning away to busy myself with a stack of papers.

The paperwork documenting this week's events doesn't need to be reorganized, but I shuffle through the pages anyway, focusing on them like they hold the secrets of the universe. Anything to keep my gaze from straying back to him.

He is not looking at me like that. I can't afford to entertain those thoughts, regardless of what Veronica said. He's so handsome. And I'm… well, I'm a thirty-five year old, nearsighted librarian with a limp and too much jiggle in my wiggle. At least that's how my Aunt Rosie would have put it. Meaning I'm on the other side of chubby.

He's young and so masculine and virile and…

"Excuse me, Ms. Burton," the deep voice says from behind me.

I squeak and then turn careful not to tangle my cane in my skirt and trip myself. He's so tall; I have to tilt my head back to see his face. And I just can't help myself as I catalogue all of his features. Those eyes that can't quite decide if they're green or brown, That smile that's part mischievous bad-boy, part boy next door. His blond hair that's a little bit shaggy on top, but trimmed on the sides and back. His white t-shirt clings to his chest and shoulders like a lover, molding to those impressive muscles. He rubs his knuckles across his cheek and I can hear the bristle of his whiskers. I want to reach up and rub his cheek too or rub my cheek against his.

What in the hell am I even thinking? And he asked me a question. Like thirty seconds ago. Or maybe even a minute and I'm just standing here staring at him like I'm an idiot.

I clear my throat, because what else do I do? "Did you need help with something?" I force myself to ask. "If you're looking for Veronica, she's shelving books in the non-fiction stacks."

His brows lower and his head shakes so infinitesimally, I almost miss it. "Who is Veronica?"

"The young woman who works up here periodically."

His mouth shifts into a half grin and it's so blinding that I'm pretty sure I see Jesus, Elvis and I now know aliens exist. "Is that library humor?"

I think back to what I said. "Oh, periodically?" I snort because yes, folks, I can get even more awkward. "Unintentional, but yes, that is good library humor."

"Callie!" Peter calls as he enters the front door. "Callie, Rory needs your help out there with her farm animals."

"Oh, of course." I grab hold of my cane and start to move away from the counter, then remember Monroe standing there. "Did you need something in particular?"

He shakes his head, his blond hair, a little long on top, flops onto his forehead. "Just going to check out these books." He sets them on the counter.

"Peter should be able to help you. I'll see you next time." I eye his stack of books and smile. "Jim Butcher is a good choice." Then I hobble my way around the counter and out the front door, not turning to see if he's watching me limp.

I hope he's not, but I'm all too aware of my uneven gait. When you're under sixty and walk with a cane, everyone watches. Everyone wonders. Usually, it doesn't bother me. I'm used to it. But today, for reasons I don't want to consider, I wish that just once I walked with the natural grace of someone who hadn't had her pelvis fractured at the age of nine.

Once I'm outside I'm met with the sounds of Rory's miniature horse and the bleats of her little goats as they hop around in the pen. There are already moms holding their kiddo's hands and looking at the animals, but they're doing their best to keep their distance since the petting zoo doesn't officially start for another twenty minutes. Rory, however, is nowhere to be seen.

I scan the small park, and then the parking lot, before I spot my friend, leaning against the side of her truck, looking positively green. I hurry towards her as quickly as I'm physically able.

"Rory, what's wrong?" I ask as soon as I reach her side.

She holds up a finger then runs behind her truck where I hear the distinct sounds of her retching.

"Oh, no," I say.

"What's wrong?" that deep voice asks from my

side. A voice that's becoming more and more familiar.

I press a palm to my chest, hoping to slow my suddenly pounding heart as I turn to face him. "I don't understand how you can be a giant and not make any noise when you move."

His brows raise and his lips quirk.

"Sorry," I say. "You just startled me."

"So what's wrong? You said, 'oh no.'"

"My friend, Aurora, Rory,"—I gesture in the direction of her truck—"Anyways, this is her petting farm and it's our activity for the kids today, but she's"—Another round of retching sounds from around the truck and I wince—"Obviously under the weather. I don't know if I can handle all the animals myself.

Rory pops up from behind her truck. "I'm so sorry, Callie."

"Sweetie, this isn't your fault. Are you okay? Do you need to go to the hospital?"

She shakes her head. "No. I think it's a touch of food poisoning."

"Why don't you turn your truck on, get the AC going and sit in there and cool off? I'll try to get you something to drink so you don't get dehydrated. And I'll figure out how to do the animals. Maybe we'll just open the bunny pen up and they can just look at the other animals?"

The kids will be so disappointed, but what can I do? I shrug.

"I'll help," Monroe says. "Let me put my books in my truck. Then I'll grab your friend a drink from the vending machine and be back to help with the animals."

I blink in surprise. "Oh, you don't have to do that."

"I know I don't. I want to. Besides, I grew up on a ranch. I've handled these kinds of animals before. Normally the larger variety, but I think I can handle it."

I give him a nod and smile. "Thank you."

"My pleasure."

It's on the tip of my tongue to comment about his nice manners. But the minute he turns around, I'm struck by the sight of his perfectly sculpted butt and the way his worn jeans mold to it. I'm surrounded by children and I am literally staring at a man's butt. Clearly, I am going to hell.

I don't have long to contemplate my future doom, because things move quickly after that. Half an hour later, Monroe is manning the goat pen and the miniature horse, and I'm safely sitting in a chair in the bunny pen while the youngest of the kids squeal and try to catch the hoppers.

"Don't pull their ears, Liam," I say. "You wouldn't like it if I pulled your ears, would you?"

He gives me a gummy grin and shakes his head.

I have to force myself to keep from staring at Monroe. He's been either in a squat position or on one knee so he's down on the level with the kids as he shows them how to feed the goats. He's patient with their questions and smiles at them, so gentle and kind. I'm in so much trouble and I'm thankful we don't have this petting zoo here every day or my ovaries would probably explode. That is if they're still awake and alive in there. Looking at Monroe certainly makes me feel like they're awake. I haven't looked at a man, felt attraction towards a man in so many years, I'd forgotten what that zing feels like when it ricochets through your belly.

At some point in the first hour, Monroe leaves the goat pen to walk Rory's pony back into the trailer. He shoots me a wink as he's coming back to the goat pen.

"The kids kept asking about the pink arm hanging from his belly," he explains with a grin.

It takes me a second to put two and two together, then I feel my eyes widen and I can't hide my own giggle. When I look back over at Monroe, he's staring at me like—well, I don't really know like what, but it stops the laugh right in my throat and I swallow it and look back at the bunnies.

By the time most of the kids have left, I swear I've got hay in my hair and bunny poop on my shoes. Thankfully Rory's food poisoning episode has passed, and while she's still a little weak, she's got some color back in her cheeks. Monroe is helping her load up all her animals and I'm standing outside telling all the kids goodbye.

"Do you think it's appropriate to have a man like him here with the children?" a snide voice asks from beside me.

I don't even have to look to know it's Miranda Dillard. We grew up together, though she's my younger brother Caleb's age. Suffice it to say, I've never liked her very much.

I don't take my eyes off of Monroe. "You mean tall, handsome, and helpful? Yeah, I can see how that would be a problem." I nod sagely. Then I go in for the kill shot. "Sure seems like Dwayne likes him a lot." Then I look over at her. Just in time to see her head swivel in that direction to see her son hanging on Monroe's every word.

"Dwayne Ulysses Dillard, you get your tail over here right now!" she shrieks.

Dwayne Ulysses? That poor kid. They gave him the initials, DUD. Why would you do that to a child?

Miranda scurries away from me.

A man like him.

"I'll call you," Rory yells out the window and then she's driving away with her truck and trailer. My phone beeps in my pocket and I pull it out to see I have a text from her.

> **Rory**: *If you don't ride that man like a carnival ride, I will never speak to you again.*
> **Me**: *I don't even know what that means.*
> **Me**: *Do not respond to this while you're driving!*

Monroe walks towards me, and I quickly pocket my phone. Thank God for the brilliant clothing designers who finally decided to start putting pockets in women's skirts.

"Thank you again for all your help. Today would have surely been a disaster without you," I tell him as he approaches.

He grins. "I had fun. It's been a while since I was around so many kids. They ask so many questions."

"About the horny pony," I say. Then I close my eyes because I cannot believe I just said that out loud to this man. Someone kill me now.

He laughs. "They would not stop asking about it and the moms were horrified."

"Well, thank you for taking care of the issue so we didn't have to have an impromptu birds and the bees discussion. That would have been a storytime to remember."

I look down and see what is undeniably poop of some origin on his jeans. I wince.

"I think you got hit." I point. "I'm pretty sure my shoes are covered in rabbit poo, but I'm sorry about your jeans."

"Don't worry about it, Buttons. It's not the first time an animal has shit on me. Probably won't be the last. You need help with anything else?" He looks around us.

Buttons? I shake my head. "No. Peter is closing up today, so I'm actually leaving soon myself. Thanks again and I'll see you around."

"You definitely will. Have a good evening." And then he turns and walks away and like the damn pervert I am, I stare at his butt again!

three

· · ·

Lone Star

Monroe

I've met my brother, Harrison, at Ruthie's Diner. It's on the square downtown, conveniently located about a block from the library. I think it's after hours for my little librarian, but still knowing I'm close to where she goes every day has me feeling aware and on edge.

Harrison isn't the most talkative of my siblings, but he's not normally this quiet and he's the one that asked me to meet him. We're halfway through our meal and he's just staring out the window between bites.

"Harrison, I'm getting older by the minute. Just talk."

He stares at me for a few breaths then rubs a hand

down his face. "You know how we said that we just need the majority of us to get married for the trust thing?"

"It just happened yesterday, brother, yeah, I remember." I remember being so fucking thankful that my siblings won't have to rely on me to get married to save our damn ranch. Would it help? Of course, but let's be honest, I'm not going to find anyone willing to marry me with my prison record.

"Here's the thing," Harrison says. "I'm kind of already married."

"Wait, what? Did this happen while I was locked up and no one told me?"

He shakes his head. "No one knows. Fuck."

"You're going to have to start at the beginning because I'm lost."

"I don't have time. I just wanted to tell you that I'm leaving town. I've got to go find her and talk to her and figure out what to do next. I'll text you as soon as I know anything."

"What do I tell the others?"

"Tell them the truth. I just didn't have time to deal with all the questions, especially since I don't have any answers yet." He pulls some cash out of his wallet and drops it on the table.

I stand up and hug him because I'm not too fucking proud to hug my siblings. You never know when you won't get to see them or touch them for months or years at a time.

"Be safe. Let me know if you need anything," I say. Then I grab his arm. "Hayes know?"

He shakes his head. "Nah. No reason for him to. I'll be back when I can."

I'm just leaving the diner when I spot a familiar shade of red hair on the park bench across the street. The town square in Saddle Creek is exactly what you would think. A square of streets lined with offices and restaurants and stores, and a beautiful green space surrounding the old limestone county courthouse. One branch of the largest live oak dips nearly to the ground, shading the park bench where the prim and proper Ms. Burton is seated.

I jog across the street and make my way across the paved path to the bench where my sexy librarian sits eating an ice cream cone. The dichotomy of her—literally—buttoned up exterior and her sensual attention to the ice cream cone ... Fuck me. It's like custom-made porn.

Her pink tongue slips out and swirls over the ice cream lapping up some of the cold treat. She's got an e-reader in her hand, and she smiles at something she's reading. That grin is like a lasso to my heart. And my legs, evidently, because I'm moving towards her faster now.

She's completely absorbed in her book and doesn't look up until my shadow falls across her reader.

I sit next to her, probably too close for two

people that don't know each other very well, but I crave her nearness. I know she's way too good for the likes of me, but I just can't help myself. I want to know everything about this woman. I want to lean closer and see what she smells like where that tender skin of her neck meets her shoulder. I want to touch those russet-colored tresses and see if they're as soft as they look. I want to kiss her mouth and see if those lips are as pillowy as they seem.

This woman has me tied up in knots and she doesn't seem to even notice.

"Hello, Mr. Crawford."

I shake my head. "Call me Roe, or Monroe if you prefer."

"All right, Roe."

"You have a little bit—" I intend to point to the small glob of ice cream at the corner of her mouth, instead I just wipe it off with my thumb. Then I bring my thumb to my lips and lick off the sweet treat. "Vanilla?"

Her lips are parted and her pupils are blown and goddamn if I don't want to press this woman against a tree and kiss the hell out of her. She swallows visibly and nods.

"I didn't mean to interrupt." I point in the opposite direction. "Do you want me to leave you to your book and ice cream?"

"No. I can read any time. And I was just about

done with this." She takes a quick lick and then stands and walks to the trashcan.

My southern boy manners fight the urge to offer to do it for her, but I sense that it would be more offensive. She might be self-conscious about her cane or her unbalanced gait, but I find her so damn sexy that it's all just a part of the woman I want to know more about.

She settles back on the bench and I'm pleased that she doesn't sit further away from me.

"What were you reading?" I ask.

"A historical romance about a woman who favors a young Queen Victoria and has to go undercover to pose as the monarch while the real queen is hidden for safety from a would-be assassination plot."

She smiles and I swear to Christ she has an honest to God twinkle in her eyes. This woman is like a Disney princess come to life. She's so sweet I'm surprised there aren't bluebirds braiding her hair.

"That sounds exciting."

"It is."

"So where's the romance come in?"

"With the royal guard protecting her. Because the assassins are still after the queen—well the fake queen—so he has to protect her which, of course means sharing one bed. In romance novels, there is always only one bed."

I shove away my mental images of sharing a bed

with Callie because right now, I just want to keep hearing her voice.

"Is romance what you mostly read?" I ask.

"No. I read a little bit of everything. But romance is my favorite. I also host a romance book club at the library two nights a month."

"Do you have a lot of members?"

"A fair number," she says with a grin.

"Any men?"

"You're welcome to come to our next meeting and see for yourself."

"Maybe I will. So when did you move to Saddle Creek?" I ask.

She looks at me and then her head falls back and she laughs. It's such a hearty, no-holds-barred, pure joyful sound that I can't help but smile back at her. She's joy personified and something in her presence soothes me; quiets that restlessness I haven't been able to rid myself of since I left the Middle East. It only got worse during my time in prison. Nothing like time in prison to think about all the blood on my hands.

I shouldn't even be talking to this woman. She's so beautiful and pure and sweet. And I'm nothing but a dirty soldier with a string of bad fucking choices behind me.

Still I can't help myself when I tell her. "You should laugh more often. I was going to tell you that at the petting zoo, but I didn't get a chance."

"Thank you."

"So why was my question funny?"

"Because I've lived here all my life."

I frown. "How is that possible? I've lived here all my life. I would have remembered you."

"Doubtful. I was homeschooled until high school and even then, I'm six years older than your older brother. I think Quinn graduated with my brother though, Caleb Burton?"

"Shit. The sheriff is your brother?"

She releases a small chuckle. "Yeah, he is."

Further proof that I did not belong sitting here with her.

"Technically not my entire life. I moved here when I was eight. Our Aunt Rosie raised us," she says. "After the car accident, at least, when our parents were killed. That's also how my hip got messed up. Anyways, that's why I was homeschooled for a while. Caleb went to school the whole time." She shakes her head. "I'm sorry. I don't know why I told you all of that."

"You can tell me anything," I admit. Her brow furrows, in what I hope is confusion, not fear. I may feel like a damn stalker, but I certainly don't want her to be afraid of me. So I explain away my admission. "I like the sound of your voice. It's soothing."

She winkles her nose. "Is that a polite way of telling me that I have a boring voice that could put you to sleep?"

I laugh. "No, not at all. I go to study at the library and get my school work turned in because our Wi-Fi out at the ranch is really slow. But I always stop what I'm doing and listen when you do storytime with the kids."

A blush spreads across her cheeks and down her throat onto the minimal part of her chest that I can see. That pretty pink skin disappears beneath her blouse and those infernal buttons. Those fucking buttons keep me up at night.

"That's very kind of you to say, Roe."

I nod. "Your Aunt Rosie, she was the librarian when we were growing up?"

A wistful smile spreads across Callie's wide mouth. "Yes. She's obviously why I became a librarian. I spent so much time in those stacks as a kid. And her house isn't much different. Caleb and I inherited that as well, but he let me have it." She lifts a shoulder. "I suppose he figures since I'll probably be an old maid like Rosie was, I should get the creepy old Victorian downtown. He has a newer ranch-style house at the edge of town. But I love my house and wouldn't trade it so I don't mind."

"Why would you be an old maid?"

Her expression changes and the blush intensifies. She stands and wobbles a bit on her feet.

I stand, too, and catch her elbow, steadying her. "Callie?"

"I need to get home."

"Do you need a ride?"

"No. It's just down the block. Have a good day." And then she walks off leaving me there, staring after her like a fool. Obviously, I made some kind of mistake, but I don't have a fucking clue what I did wrong.

I rub at the back of my hair. "Fuck." I follow behind her, at a distance, just to make sure she gets home safely. I know where her Aunt Rosie lived. I don't mean to be a creeper, but I clearly upset her and I just want to make sure she's okay.

When I see her climb the three steps up to the wrap-around porch of the massive white Victorian house, I turn around and head for my truck. It's probably for the best. Callie Burton is way too good for a man like me.

She wants romance and love and sweetness and all I have to offer is filthy, sweaty sex and plenty of orgasms. I'd keep her safe, but hell, her brother is the sheriff so she clearly doesn't need me for that.

"Evening, Monroe."

Speak of the fucking devil. I turn to face her brother and he's decked out in all his sheriff gear, his hand resting on the handle of his baton.

"Sheriff," I say, inclining my head.

"I understand you've been spending quite a bit of time at the library these days. Any particular reason?"

"As a matter of fact, yes. They have a great selection of books, which I appreciate. And their Wi-Fi is faster than mine at home."

"Any other reason?"

"What are you asking me, Sheriff?" I ask.

"Just that I hear you've been visiting with my sister on more than one occasion." He nods over to the bench where Callie and I were just sitting.

"Your sister is a grown woman."

"And you are convicted felon."

His words pour over me like a bucket of iced water. "I hear your message. Loud and clear."

"I'm glad we understand each other."

I nod and walk to my truck. It was a good reminder. I might want Callie Burton, but I sure as fuck don't deserve her.

four

. . .

Callie

I've just sat down on my couch with a big bowl of buttered popcorn and a queued up episode of *True Murder* when my phone rings.

I already know it's Rory. The only two people who call me are her and my brother. And I already had to deal with a call from him earlier. I smile at the picture of the baby goat face on my screen.

"Hello, Rory."

"You do not sound nearly excited enough to be the woman on the receiving end of Mr. Tall, Blond and Sexy's flirting."

My silly heart pounds at her words, but I ruthlessly squash the feeling. Of course, he flirts with me. He's a flirt. I'm sure he treats every woman that way.

Because it can't possibly be me. "I don't know what you're talking about."

"Girl, Jesus himself is going to come down and smite you for lying like that. Tell me you didn't notice the way he looked at you and helped you?"

"He was helping the library and the kids."

I can actually hear her eyes rolling over the phone.

"Callie Louise Burton, I'm going to drive myself over there and give you a stern talking to."

I smile because there is no one in the world like Rory. She might be younger than me, but she is the best friend I've had. "Louise is not my middle name."

"Whatever. Not the point. Seriously, Cal, you have to have noticed," she says, her voice more gentle this time.

I exhale a slow breath. "Yes, I've noticed. But before you get all crazy excited and start thinking it's something it's not, I'm sure he's like that with every woman. Some southern boys are just charming that way."

"He wasn't like that with me," she snaps.

"You were vomiting."

"Fair point. Does he flirt with the other women in the library? All the moms?"

He didn't know who Veronica was when I asked him. And I've never seen him look at any of the other women. I think back to earlier on the park bench when he wiped that bit of ice cream off my mouth then licked if off his thumb. It was the single most erotic thing I've ever seen. But I'm definitely not going to tell Rory about it. Instead I swing the conversation in a slightly different direction.

"Caleb called me earlier to warn me to 'stay away from Monroe Crawford because he's not the sort of man I should associate with.'"

She snorts. "He would. Your brother acts like he's the older sibling."

"Don't I know it?"

"What did you tell him?"

"To mind his own business. That I was an adult and I could associate with whomever I wanted."

Rory laughs. "Listen, I know you don't read the *Saddle Peek*," Rory says, mentioning the town's gossip social media page. It's still run like an old school bulletin board style page, but it is the best and fastest source of town information.

"No, I don't read it. If it's worth anything, I'll hear about it at the library tomorrow." I made the mistake once of going on there, eager for the juicy gossip of our small town and found an old thread about the poor, sweet librarian. Never again.

"I didn't figure. So the hottest news tonight is that all six of the Crawford kids have to get married or lose their ranch and some other bigger property to our north."

A jab of pain slices through me, but it's ridiculous

to feel sad at the thought of Monroe Crawford getting married. I have no claim on that man. I'm nearly a decade older than him. I have literally nothing to offer.

"Why are you telling me this?" I ask.

"Because I figure you can do one of two things," Rory says. But then she pauses.

"Which are?"

"You can have a hot steamy hookup with him before he gets himself hitched or you can offer to marry him yourself."

At that I burst out laughing.

"What is so funny? Callie, I'm totally serious."

"Me? You want me to offer to marry that … that man? Have you seen him, Rory? Have you seen me? We do not match. He drips sexy. I mean it oozes out of his pores for heaven's sake. And I'm ten years older than him. Let's not even talk about my body."

"What's the matter with your body? Curvy is in, sweet thing, real men love women with some meat on their bones."

"I even believe that, if the curves come in a package like yours. You're proportionate. A perfect hourglass."

"With more sand than is conventionally deemed acceptable."

"Right. But my curves, if that's what we have to call them, are none of those things. My hips and thighs and butt are too big and my boobs are too small for a woman my size. I haven't even mentioned my scars or my limp and cane."

"Callie, I've seen how that man looks at you, he doesn't seem at all bothered by your disproportionate curves. He's attracted to you. What could it hurt to put yourself out there? You know, he might be sex on legs, but he's not perfect either. There are plenty of narrow minded women in this town who wouldn't touch him regardless of how hot he is."

"Because of his prison stint? Yes, I know." I'm not quite able to keep my derision from my voice as I remember Miranda Dillard's silliness.

But Rory must take my tone to mean something else, because she asks, "Does it bother you?"

"Honestly? No, it doesn't," I say quickly. "But—okay, I'm going to admit something here, and you can't give me any crap about it."

"Promise."

"After he started coming to the library, there were whispers. Then, of course, my brother had to call me and warn me of how potentially dangerous he was. So I put my librarian skills to work and researched him. I read the case file, as much of it was public, at least. He settled. It never went to court. As best I can tell, it was nothing more than a tragic accident, but the district attorney was hell-bent on making an example out of him."

"That's crap."

I exhale slowly. "I haven't spent very much time

with him at all, just a handful of short conversations, but I've never seen even a hint of anger or violence or anything like that. He's so sweet with the kids, too. He's always there at storytime, and even though he's trying to get his own work done, inevitably some kid will interrupt him, but he's patient and sweet with them."

"Sounds like he'd make a good father."

Her words are like a kick to my gut and something resonates in them.

"Did the post about the Crawfords say how much time they have before they all have to get married?" I ask.

"Not in so many words, but it sounds like an ASAP kind of situation. And six of them! Can you imagine? Of course, they're all hot so it shouldn't be too hard," Rory says.

"Well, why don't you pick one?" I ask.

She snorts. "I don't think so. I have my hands full enough with all my animals. I mean an extra pair of hands would be helpful for that. And the occasional orgasm that I don't have to provide myself."

I laugh. "TMI, crazy lady."

"How are you still this shy at thirty-five?"

"Shut up. I'm not shy. I just don't see the purpose of openly discussing masturbation."

She clicks her tongue. "Maybe I should buy you a toy."

"You wouldn't."

"I could have it delivered to the library."

"Aurora, I will murder you and bury you in your composting bin."

She cackles. "Fair enough. I'll keep my toys to myself."

"Toys, plural? Oh my gosh, how many do you have?" She starts to answer, but I stop her. "No! Never mind, I don't actually want to know."

"Fine. Talk to you tomorrow?"

"Always."

"Love you, Callie-Lou-Who."

"Love you too, Rory-Borealis."

We hang up, and I stare at the streaming service icon bouncing around on my TV screen and then down at my now soggy and cold popcorn.

Like he'd make a good father.

My thoughts bop around in my head, faster than the bouncing logo. I stand and know that if I'm going to do this, I have to do it now, because if not, I'll make a thousand excuses tomorrow and maybe miss my one chance. I grab my car keys and purse, then stop at the mirror in my dining room. I put on a little lip gloss and pinch my cheeks and wipe under my eyes so maybe I don't look so tired. But you know what? He's seen me before. It's not like he doesn't know that I'm far from a beauty queen.

Before I pull out of my driveway, I check the *Saddle Peek* and read up on all the posts regarding the Crawford siblings. If the rumors are to be believed then they do need to be married, all of them and soon.

Maybe Roe already has a girlfriend, but maybe he doesn't. And if he doesn't, then I could help him with his problem and he … well, he could finally give me what I've wanted for years.

five

. . .

Lone Star Ex-Con

Monroe

"Roe! Get your ass down here; you've got a visitor," Quinn yells from the living room.

I've just gotten out of the shower and I've got a towel on my head and one around my waist. I pull on some jeans and try to dry my hair as best I can as I pad my way from my bedroom to the main living area. This old house still looks the same as it did when we were kids. It's a sprawling two story Arts and Crafts Foursquare that my mom's grandparents built back in the twenties. It's been renovated several times over the years, as more rooms were added on to accommodate all the kids and the appliances updated. Of course, it's not as clean as it was when Mama was alive, and no house that's almost a hundred years old has enough bathrooms, but we get by.

Most recently, the kitchen was opened up and a living area was added on to the back of the house. That's where I find Quinn, sitting in his favorite chair with a long neck dangling from two fingers. I raise my brows to my brother.

He nods toward the front of the house. "She wanted to wait outside on the porch."

"She?"

"Yup." He grins, but doesn't give me any more than that.

I toss my towel at him and go out the door, the screen door slams behind me. And there's Callie.

"Callie, hi."

Her copper eyes eat up my naked torso, slow, slow, slow. Like she's a master cartographer and she's mapping out every contour and line. I step closer to her and that seems to break whatever spell she was under because her eyes flick to my face and she blushes.

"Sorry. I didn't mean to show up here unannounced, but I didn't have your number." Then, she adds in a rush, "And I wouldn't have called anyways because the truth is I knew if I didn't do this tonight, and do it in person, then I'd lose whatever bravado I seem to be running on and I'd never ask."

"Okay." God she's cute when she's nervous. "Do

you want something to drink? Or we could go inside? Sit somewhere?"

"Let's sit over there." She points to the darkness off the porch where I know that double swing hangs from the big oak limb.

"Yeah, sounds good," I say.

I grab her elbow to lead her over there since it's dark and I don't want her to stumble on a tree root or anything else. We sit and swing in silence for a few minutes. The sounds of cicadas and tree frogs serenade us and I finally understand why Mama and Daddy came out here all the time and sat on this old swing, holding hands and talking. It's romantic out here.

"Callie, is everything okay? Are you in some kind of trouble?"

"No. It's nothing like that. Wow, this is harder than I thought." She blows out a breath. "Okay, I'm just gonna rip off the proverbial bandage. I heard through the good ol' Saddle Creek rumor mill that you and your siblings have to get married because of some issue with your grandfather's will."

I sit back and chuckle. "Damn, word does travel fast here. I'd forgotten about that. Yes, that's all true."

She turns her body to face me just as the moon peeks out from behind some clouds and her face is illuminated. She looks so damn beautiful, I want to write a poem or paint her face, despite the fact that I have neither of those skills. This woman has me tied up in knots.

A furrow appears between her brows. "Do you have a girlfriend? Or have you already found who you're going to marry?" she asks.

"No. I've been gone for a while. First the Army and then… " I trail off.

She licked her lips.

She makes it damned hard to concentrate. "Why do you ask?"

Her eyes squeeze shut. "I was thinking we could come to an agreement. An arrangement or trade or whatever you want to call it." Those copper eyes land on my face searching. "More than anything in the world, Roe, I want to be a mother." Those gorgeous eyes fill with tears as she speaks and a knot tightens my throat. "If I married you, I mean I know there are no guarantees, and maybe the idea of marrying me or being with me is not at all what you want, but I thought I would offer."

I cup her cheek just as a tear slides down. I thumb it away. "Ah, Buttons, you don't want to marry me."

She tries to stand and move away from me, but I keep her in place.

"Just a minute. Let me explain. There are things about me that you don't know."

"You can just tell me no, Roe. I get it. I'm older than you and well I've never been any man's fantasy."

"You're *my* fantasy. You would turn eight different shades of red if I told you all the filthy things I've thought about doing to you."

She licks her lips and I swallow a groan.

I close my eyes and steel myself for her disgust, for when she hears the truth about me and turns and walks away. She'll probably ban me from the library. Or at least from storytime.

"I'm a convicted felon, Callie. I went to prison for killing a man."

"You went to prison for involuntary manslaughter which is a second degree felony," she says.

"You know?"

"Small town, Roe. Of course I know. I would love to hear the story from your mouth because I don't trust other people's interpretations though."

I scrub a hand down my face. "I'd just gotten out of the Army, on a medical discharge for a piece of shrapnel that is permanently lodged in my arm. My arm twitched constantly when it first happened and then for months after the wound healed. I can't feel it, but it's there and it effectively ended my military career. I was over in Austin visiting some buddies and we were leaving a bar. I'd had one beer. Anyways, there was a couple arguing in the parking lot and the guy was clearly roughing the woman up, grabbing her arms and shaking her. So I went over and told him to let her go or I'd call the cops. He told me to fuck off and continued to squeeze that woman's arms. I know she had to have had perfect impressions of his fingerprints bruised into her skin the next day. Anyways, I tried again; told him to let her go. He turned around and came at me and I shoved him away. He lost his footing and fell backwards into the concrete parking curb. Cracked his skull open and," I shake my head, "he never regained consciousness."

"Didn't the woman tell the police what happened?"

"She said I shoved her husband down and he'd had no chance with me since I'm such a huge guy. She wasn't wrong. He wasn't even five foot nine."

"But you pled guilty to manslaughter. It was an accident."

"Yes and yes, but the DA made it very clear that since I'd been in special operations, I had unique skills. I was essentially a walking, talking weapon. Add that to my size and—" I shrug.

"You didn't deserve to go to prison for that, Roe."

Her voice is gentle and I want to bathe in it. I want her to tell me every day for the rest of my life that I'm forgiven, but I can't ask that of her.

"I killed men over there too, Buttons. They trained me to be a killing machine."

She shakes head. "No, they trained you to be a soldier and you did your job. And now you're home and it's time to stop punishing yourself. So if you don't want to marry me for any other reason than your criminal background, just be honest."

"You would still marry me? Have a baby with me?" I ask.

"Yes, that's why I came out here. Besides, I think I'd be getting the better end of the deal."

"I don't think so, baby." I cup her face and do the thing I've want to do since the first moment I laid eyes on her. I kiss her. I don't devour her; now isn't the right time for that. I just sip at her lips because she's the finest of wines, so rich and delicate.

Little open mouthed nibbles across her lips and she gives them right back to me. And I want to pull her into my lap and let her feel how hard she gets me. I kiss her pillowy lips, so soft, so lush, then I press my forehead to hers.

"I would love, more than anything, to marry you, Callie Burton."

six

Lone Star

Monroe

I wait until Callie's car lights are completely gone before I go back inside. Quinn is still sitting in the same spot.

"What was all that about? You sweet on the librarian?"

I sit on the edge of the couch and smile at my older brother. "As a matter of fact, I am. And I'm gonna marry her."

"That's fast," Quinn says.

"Didn't you say we needed to get married?"

"Yeah, but you said no one would have you because you're a big, bad criminal," he says that last bit with an annoying childish voice.

"I do not talk like that."

"You do know that her brother is the sheriff and he's going to shit a monkey when he finds out you two are getting hitched?"

My lips quirk in a smile because that image is fucking hilarious. But he's right. "I plan to go talk to him tomorrow."

"Think that's wise?"

"Probably not. But I think it's the honorable thing to do."

He nods. "Did you see Harrison's message in the Jolly Ranchers?"

"I did."

"Fucking coward to drop that bomb after he'd already left town."

I take a deep breath. "He told me before he left so he wasn't a complete coward."

"Did he tell you who he's married to?"

"Nope."

"Secretive fucker."

I chuckle. "You just don't like being the last to know things."

He flips me off. "I'm going to hire a housekeeper. I'm tired of this place looking like three bachelors live here. And it's just gonna get worse when Johnny gets home this summer." He tilts his chin up. "Think your girlfriend would let us post a flyer up or something at the library?"

"Fiancee, not girlfriend. Which reminds me, I

need to go buy a ring tomorrow before I see her brother."

"She moving into your bedroom?"

"No. She owns that old Victorian off the square. Remember Rosie, the librarian from when we were kids? That's her old place. Callie is her niece."

He nods. He's quiet for a minute before he asks, "She going to make you happy, brother?"

"Yeah, she is."

"Good, you deserve it after everything you've endured. Just make sure you still get your ass out here and get your work done and we won't have a problem. These cows can't take care of themselves."

He gets up to leave the room, then pauses. "Oh and Roe, when it comes time for the fucking prenup, use Blake. I went and filled him in on everything and he's created a template already for each of us. You remember where his office is?"

My stomach tightens. Blake was Quinn's best friend and the lawyer I used when I was arrested. He's not a criminal attorney, which he'd told me repeatedly, and he apologized profusely for how things went down. But all of it was my choice. He's a good guy. I just don't like remembering that whole ordeal.

"Yeah. I'll go see him."

seven

. . .

Callie

The library is unusually slow today and I'm so antsy, I'm going insane. If I had the body for it, I'd run up and down the stacks just to get rid of some of this pent up energy. But I think my hip would punish me if I tried that.

The doors open and I turn to see Roe's sister come in. I've seen her before, met her a couple of times, but not since becoming engaged to her brother. Though maybe he hasn't told any of his siblings that yet.

I smile at her.

"Hey Callie, you have anyone to watch the desk for you?"

"Sure, why?" My heart pounds and nerves curdle

the contents of my stomach. Has something happened to him?

"I just saw Roe go into your brother's office and I figure you might want to mediate that encounter in case things go sideways."

"Oh shit," I murmur. "Peter, I need you to close up for me." I grab my purse and follow Madison out without a backwards glance.

The Sheriff's Office is located just up the block and on the opposite side of the street. The closer we get, the more I can hear the flow of the river just beyond.

"So you and my brother, huh?" Madison asks with a grin.

"Monroe," I say to clarify.

She laughs. "I guess I do have a lot of brothers, but yeah, that one." She leans a little closer and lowers her voice. "He's my favorite though."

"Do the others know?"

"Probably. I don't try very hard to hide it."

"I guess I'm glad I never had to choose a favorite. It's always just been me and Caleb."

We make it to the front door of the county Sheriff's Offices. One pull on that door and we're met with a whoosh of refrigerated air.

"Good Lord, they could hang meat in here," Madison says.

I'm just about to comment, but I hear my brother's angry voice coming from his office. I hurry my pace.

"Uh-oh," Madison says. "That doesn't sound good."

"I can handle my brother," I tell her.

She smiles widely at me. "Then I'm glad I'm here to watch."

"Look, I know you got the shaft on your conviction," Caleb says. "I get that you didn't mean for it to go down that way, but I also know that prison changes people. I can't risk that for my sister. She's delicate. And she deserves better than you."

"You're right about one thing," Roe says. "She does deserve better than me. But your sister isn't some delicate flower, she's strong and brave and beautiful."

I storm into the room—well, I do whatever is similar to storming when you walk unevenly and with the assistance of a cane. "Nice to know that the men folk are here making all the choices for me since I'm too damn delicate to do it for myself."

"Now Callie, that's not what I meant," my brother says.

I point at him. "Sit down and be quiet."

He frowns and his jaw tightens, but he does exactly what I say. Though before his bottom hits his chair, he sees Madison behind me and he tips his head. "Miss Crawford. Nice to see you."

"Sheriff," she says."

"Callie, I had this under control," Roe says in a low voice.

I raise my brows at him. "Yes, that's exactly what it sounded like down the hall." I stare at the chair behind him. "You can sit down too."

He licks his lips and there's a ghost of grin that plays at the corners. But he sits all the same.

"I'm not sure if you're aware of this, little brother," I say, emphasizing the last two words. "But I am a fully grown adult. I even went to college and got two degrees. I run a library and even manage to supervise both full-time and part-time employees. I've served on town and church committees and I am fully capable of deciding when and with whom I wish to marry."

"I understand that, Callie, but it's not that simple. There are things you don't know," Caleb says.

I raise my brows. "What? Like his second degree felony? The fact that he pled guilty? The fact that he'll be on parole and can't go into bars for five years? Or is it the fact that I'm nearly a decade older than him? Precisely what is it that you think I don't know?"

My brother's mouth flattens into a tight line. "He doesn't seem like the right guy for you."

"Thank you for expressing your opinion, now I'm going to tell you how things are going to go," I say. "I've made my choice." I reach down beside me where Roe sits and he grabs my hand, twining our fingers together. He squeezes my hand. "I'm going to marry Roe. I would appreciate your support. Even more than that, I'd love for you to walk me down the aisle or whatever you call it at the courthouse because even though I'm annoyed with you at the moment you're still my brother and I love you. I'd like you at my wedding."

Caleb takes a shuddering breath and then nods as if he's resigning himself to what I've said. "Okay, Callie Mae, I'll be there. You tell me the time and I'll be there." He stands and walks around his desk and hugs me. Then like the good man I know he can be he extends a hand out to Roe.

"Before I say welcome to the family, I have to say that if you ever lay a hand on my sister," his other hand goes to his gun secured in his belt, "It will be a justifiable homicide."

Roe stands and takes Caleb's outstretched hand. "If I ever lose my mind and lay a hand on Callie, I give you permission to take me out." Then Roe is behind me, gripping both of my biceps. "This woman is a treasure and I fully intend on treating her as one."

His words warmed me. I knew they were for the benefit of my brother and I tried to tell my silly heart not to cling to them. But hearts are silly for a reason. Especially hopeful romantic hearts like mine.

Roe takes my hand and pulls me out of my brother's office. He leans down a little. "I have something for you."

My heart is pounding so furiously it's a wonder he can't hear it or see it through my sweater. "I smile up at him. Is it the prenup? Because I already told you that I don't want your money. I have my own."

"No, Buttons, it's not the prenup. I'll have that ready for us both to sign right before the ceremony. Please know that I'd never ask for such a thing if given the choice. It's just my mean as a rattler grandfather. And it's not about the money, it's the land and—"

I stop and turn to him, reaching up and cupping his face. "Roe, stop. I know, and I don't care. None of that matters to me."

We're just outside the Sheriff's Office building and Roe has me backed up to the brick. He kisses me, his lips soft and gentle. The bristles of his whiskers scratch my skin. God help me, but it makes me think of that short cropped beard scraping against more tender skin.

And then he's gone. My eyes flutter open to find him on one knee in front of me.

"Roe, that's not necessary. Seriously, the whole town—"

"Callie Burton, you've put me under a spell and I'd be forever grateful if you'd agree to be my wife." Then he holds up a ring.

I smile widely at him and ignore the tears

streaming down my face because even though this is a sham of a proposal for a sham of a marriage, that was beautiful. He makes me feel beautiful—and wanted.

He jumps to his feet. "I could have bought you a brand new ring, but this one just looked like you. If you don't like it, we can exchange it. Mr. Temple said it was from the turn of the century."

I look down at the gold band that's shaped like a vine with tiny leaves that come off of it. Each leaf is studded with a small emerald. Then the center stone is a ruby. "It's gorgeous."

"I know it's not a traditional engagement ring," he says.

"No, it's perfect. I love it so much." I never knew such a ring existed, but had I known, it would have been my choice, my dream engagement ring. And he'd just known.

He slides it on my left finger and it fits perfectly. "I can't wait until tomorrow and I can call you my wife."

eight

...

Monroe

There was no time for me to pack much more than an overnight bag so that's all I have with me. It's slung over my shoulder as I'm blatantly staring at my wife's—my wife's!—ass while she unlocks the front door.

"I'll get you a key made tomorrow," she says, looking over her shoulder. She finally gets the door opened, but I grab hold of the back of her dress to halt her movements.

"Wait right there, Buttons. We've got to do this right." I drop my bag and swing her up in my arms. "A man has to carry his bride across the threshold on their wedding day."

"Roe, that's unnecessary. I'm far too heavy."

"I've hauled feed bags that weigh more than you." Still I set her down as soon as we enter the house, mostly because she's uncomfortable, but also because this room has built-in bookshelves everywhere. "Wow."

"Wait until you see the actual library," she says.

"There's a library in the house?"

"Of course. What dusty old Victorian home isn't equipped with a library?" She nudges my shoulder. "It even has one of those rolling ladders for the higher shelves."

"That's so cool. Were these all your aunt's?"

"More or less in the library. I've replaced most of the ones in here with my favorites. You can borrow whatever."

I grab my bag off the porch and shut and lock the door.

"Would you like a tour now or later?" she asks.

I grab her by the hips. "Later. We have more important matters to attend to."

She twists out of my arms. "Oh, well, I'm not ovulating at the moment, so we don't have to do anything now. Did you want a schedule of my cycle or do you want me to just tell you when?" She walks out of the room and I follow her. "I use an app on my phone and I bet I could add it to your phone and it would sync and then you would—"

I spin her around and press her body against the

wall of whatever hallway we're in. "Callie, what are you doing?"

"Just trying to make things easier on you?"

"On me? Or on you?"

She frowns. "What do you mean?"

"Well, you're putting an awful lot of barriers in place to keep me from your promised land, Buttons. So my question is this, do you not want to have sex with me?"

She opens her mouth and then closes it. Once. Twice. A third time.

"Or are you making excuses for me because you're under some misguided assumption that I'm not attracted to you?"

She swallows and looks down at the floor.

"Ah, so that's it. I see." I lean forward and slide my nose up the side of her throat, just to inhale her sweet, sweet skin. I can't even put a name to her scent; it's just her, my Callie, and it's perfect. "Do you know why I've been calling you, Buttons?"

Her "no" comes outs a hoarse whisper.

"Every time I see you in the library you're wearing these prim little skirts and these button-up blouses with those cardigans, again with those tiny buttons. So many buttons." I reach between us and unbutton my jeans, then lower the zipper. My rock hard cock thanks me that it's no longer being imprinted with the metal teeth. "Goddamn, baby, the number of times I've had to recite the names of the states and capitols just to get my mind off you and those fucking buttons. It's inappropriate for a grown man to get a hard-on in the public library when the sexy, buttoned-up librarian is reading to children."

She sucks in a breath, but I know she's not offended. No, I can see the blush on her cheeks and spreading down her chest, disappearing into her cleavage. And I can see how the blacks of her pupils are swallowing the copper color of her eyes. She wants me too.

Thank fuck.

I grab her hand and bring it to the front of my boxers so she can feel my erection. "If there's ever a moment that you don't want me, you say the word and I'll back off. But never, ever think that I don't want you."

Her fingers curve around my dick.

"Do you understand me, Callie?"

"Yes." She licks her lips and I take advantage of the movement to lean down and steal her mouth in a heated kiss. This time I don't hold back.

I lick my tongue into her mouth, groaning when she matches my fervor. Goddamn, but this woman was made just for me.

Her fingers start searching for the waistband on my boxers, but I grab her hand.

"You touch me now, baby, and this will be over way too fast. I want you too badly." I look around the hall and the stairs. "Where's the bedroom?"

"You can pick whichever one you want."

"Woman, I'm tempted to put you over my lap and spank that plump ass of yours until it's as red as your hair. Where is *OUR* bedroom?"

She nods her head down the hallway to her right.

I pick her up in a fireman hold and carry her down the hall, then I let her slide down my body.

"Callie Crawford. I like the sound of that. What do you think?"

"It's nice." She bites down on her lip. "Are you really going to spank me?"

"Depends. You going to keep trying to push me away and make me sleep somewhere you're not?"

"I guess not."

I tilt my head back. "She guesses not." I unbutton my white dress shirt and toss it into a hamper of clothes I see in the corner. I do the same with the undershirt I'm wearing. I toe off my boots and then pull off my jeans and socks leaving me in my tight black boxer briefs. They're obscene right now because I'm so fucking hard. I look down. "That's ridiculous," I murmur, pointing to my erection. "Looks like I'm pitching a tent for *The Borrowers*."

Her mouth falls open and then she bursts out laughing. She giggles for a while and then wipes her eyes. "You're terrible."

"Maybe, but I got you to relax." I grab her arms, rubbing my hands up and down the smooth exposed skin. "Even in this dress, you've got tiny little buttons. You're like a present I want to unwrap, again and again."

I start at the top button and slip it through the hole, then repeat with the next one. But the time I've reached the fourth button I can see her shear bra and my mouth is watering. Another few buttons and the dress is loose enough to slip off her hips and pool at her feet.

I suck in my breath and stare at the woman before me, my wife and the object of my fantasies for the last several weeks. She's even better than I imagined.

"You're so pretty, my sweet wife." I sit on the edge of the bed and pull her to stand between my thighs. I'm so damn tall that this puts me at eye level with her tits. Perfect, rose-tipped beauties that are going to fit in my mouth like they were made to be there.

"We don't match," she says.

"Of course we don't. We're not supposed to. Women are supposed to be soft." I grip her thighs and pull her forward, encouraging her to straddle my lap. She comes willingly and those pale thighs across my darker ones are like a jolt to my dick. Is there anything about this woman that doesn't turn me on?

I slide my thumb across the front of her panties and realize that she's already soaked through the white cotton.

"Look how much you need me, Buttons. Have

you been wanting me every day the way I've been wanting you?"

She nods.

"Have you come home and slid your hand up that prim little librarian skirt, parted those slick folds and fingered yourself to the thought of me?

She whimpers, but nods.

"Fuck." I kiss her and move my hand in a steady rhythm. I'm not even inside her panties yet, just a subtle, but steady rub-rub against the outside of her clit.

Her noises increase and she pulls away from our kiss too distracted to continue.

"Roe, please don't stop."

"I'm never gonna stop, baby."

Then she shatters and it's the most beautiful thing I've ever seen. And I come in my goddamn boxers like a horny teenager.

"Look what you did to me, Buttons. I made a mess all over myself." I pick her up and set her gently on the bed, then stand and pull off my boxers. I clean off the rest of my come with a dry part of my underwear, then toss them into the hamper across the room.

"Oh, I didn't mean to," she says, but her eyes are glued to my cock and she's licking her lips. She doesn't look terribly apologetic.

I laugh. "Don't worry. This is a perk of marrying a younger man. I'll be hard again in a few minutes.

Let's get you naked the rest of the way though because I'm not done playing with your gorgeous body."

She reaches behind her and unhooks her bra, letting it fall off her shoulders. Her breasts are teardrop shaped and the palest of pale skin. Her areolas are small and barely a shade darker, but her nipples are large and bold and demand my immediate attention. I lean forward and catch one between my lips, flicking my tongue against it.

She hisses out a breath. I play with her tits a while longer with my mouth and hands until she's moaning and writhing around on the bed. By now I'm rock hard again. I move between her thighs and pull her panties down and off her legs.

She's not a waxer, no, my girl is far too practical for that. Not to mention old fashioned. She does trim though and the tidy triangle of red curls that meets my gaze makes my dick jump.

I spread her thighs and then part her lips. She's glossy with her arousal, sticky with need. Her musky scent hits my nose and I breathe her in.

"Oh Buttons, you're gonna be the death of me. I gotta taste you and then, then I'm going to fuck you."

"Oh wow," she says.

I slide down onto my belly and wedge my shoulders between her thighs. Normally I'd start with her clit, but I gotta taste that sweet nectar so instead I plunge my tongue directly into her tight channel.

She bucks up towards my mouth and shrieks. So sweet and responsive.

"I could eat you for hours," I tell her.

"I think you'd kill me."

I alternate my moves, fucking her with my tongue and then sliding up to suck on her clit. She's not quiet, and I love it. I slide one finger up inside her, hook it, and wait for her reaction to let me know if I've found the magic spot.

"Oh God, oh wow," she says.

Okay, right spot. She's so goddamn wet, my finger fucking in and out of her makes an obscene noise. And it just makes me harder. Precum leaks from the tip of my cock, and I moan against her pussy.

Her fingers grab onto my short hair and hold my face firmly to her.

"Oh, oh, oh, oh fuck!" she yells. "I'm gonna come. Oh God, I'm gonna come so hard." Then her pussy clenches down on my finger, squeezing me while she calls out my name.

I give her a kiss on her belly, then lean up. I wipe my face on my forearm, then take my time crawling up her body, kissing her everywhere. Her belly button, the scar on her injured hip, each hard pink nipple, her sweet smelling neck, and then finally her mouth.

I grip my cock and rub it through her slick folds, coating myself in her arousal. "You're so damn wet,

Buttons. So fucking perfect. I can't wait any longer."

"Don't wait."

"Will you let me know if I hurt you?" I grab her scarred hip gently so she knows what I mean.

She nods.

I enter her slowly, reveling in how hot and wet and slick her pussy is. It's like she was custom-made for me. I bottom out and she groans.

"So full."

"Too much?"

"No, it's good. I'm just really full." She bends up her good leg and hooks it over my waist and it opens her pussy up so that when I start to pump in and out, I know I'll grind against her clit.

I go slow, withdrawing, and then pushing back in. Shallow at first.

"You feel fucking amazing," I say.

"Stop treating me like I'm going to break. You don't need to hold back with me, Roe. Take me the way you want to."

How she knew I was holding back, I'll never know, but I nod. I reposition myself so I'm on my knees; it'll give me greater control without putting too much weight on her. Plus I get to see her whole body this way.

This time when I withdraw and push back in, I don't hold back. And it feels amazing.

Her eyes roll up and she bites down on her lip.

She reaches up and cups her tits, flicking at her nipples.

"You're so sexy, baby. Fuck you feel good. So tight and wet. Goddamn, you're squeezing my dick."

Then her eyes go wide, and her mouth falls open. "I can't." She shakes her head. "So good, it's so damn good."

I thrust again, pulling nearly all the way out, then slamming back in again. And again. And again.

"Roe!" Her head tilts back as she screams my name. Her pussy squeezes and pulses around me triggering my own orgasm. She milks my cock with every pulse and I swear I've never come so hard.

"Yes, Callie. Oh, my sweet, sweet, Callie."

nine

. . .

Callie

I stare down at my ring, my eyes swimming with tears. I've been Roe's wife all of two weeks. And it's been so amazing, I can't even believe it's my life. He doesn't let a night go by without making love to me. He grabs me and kisses me for no reason. Sits next to me on the couch and holds my hand while we both read or he reads while I watch one of my true crime shows.

Frankly, I don't understand how this is my life. I know many of the town people don't get it either. I see their stares and whispers. They don't understand how the frumpy, disabled librarian landed the ridiculously hot, younger cowboy. Get in line, people, I don't understand it either.

Only I do.

He needed a wife for the trust. I offered and he accepted. I'm a willing body and most men like sex. It's not all that complicated, I suppose. Still, after my doctor's appointment, I have to come clean and tell him the truth. If he walks away, it will break my heart because I am already wholeheartedly in love with that man, but I will also completely understand.

I hear his truck door slam outside the carport and I swipe at my eyes.

"Buttons, I'm home," he greets from the front door. His boots tap-tap-tap through the house until he finds me, sitting in the dark at the dining room table. "What are you doing in here alone and in the dark, baby?" He flicks on the lights.

I see the flowers in his hands, a huge bouquet of Texas wildflowers: Bluebonnets, Indian Blankets, Mexican Hats, Buttercups, Winecups, Indian Paintbrushes. He sets them on the table, forgotten and kneels in front of me.

Those big hands of his cup my face. "Why is my beautiful girl crying? What happened?"

"We have to talk. Sit down, Roe."

He frowns. "I don't like the sound of that."

"Just let me get it all out."

He grabs one of the chairs and pulls it right in front of mine.

"I went to the doctor."

He immediately goes sheet white.

I shake my head. "No, I'm fine. It's nothing like that."

His eyes close and relief washes over him. "Christ, baby, you scared the fuck out of me." He leans over and presses a kiss to my cheek and then another to my forehead.

"So I went to the doctor and because of my advanced age, I'm considered geriatric." I sniff and will the tears not to start again. "By the Obstetricians. So if I got pregnant, and that's a big if, then it would be risky. And it might not even happen because apparently my eggs are old." I've lost the fight with the tears.

Roe stands and I think he's just going to walk out, and my heart cracks. But then he scoops me out of my chair and carries me into the living room where he settles us onto the couch. He pulls me into his lap.

"I need you close to me when you're sad, Buttons. I need to hold you."

"Okay." I sniff. "Anyways, they said all of this and I realized that I jumped the gun. I married, you so you could give me a baby, but I might not even be able to have kids. And now I'm robbing you of a younger wife. One who isn't geriatric with rotten eggs."

He chuckles.

"I'm serious, Roe."

"What are you saying then?"

"I think we should get an annulment. I think you should be free to find a better choice."

He stares at me for several moments and I can't tell what he's thinking. He's frowning and his jaw is tight, so he doesn't seem too happy.

"I'm sorry if this messes with the timeline for your trust or whatever."

"Do you remember when the judge asked us what kind of ceremony we wanted? Whether or not we wanted to do our own vows or if we wanted to do traditional vows?"

"Yes."

"And I specifically asked that we do the traditional vows. Do you know why?"

"You're a traditional guy?" I ask with a shrug.

"No. Because I wanted to say those words to you. I'm going to say them again now. So listen closely."

I'm sobbing now and probably look like a snotty mess, but this man, oh, how I love this man.

"I, Monroe Crawford, take you, Callie Burton, to be my lawfully wedded wife, to have and to hold."

His blue eyes lock onto mine and I listen to the deep gravel of his voice.

"From this day forward; for better, for worse, for richer, for poorer, in sickness and in health." He holds up a finger. "And I'll add for emphasis. "That sickness and health includes geriatric wives and old rotten eggs."

I release a watery laugh.

He cups my face and locks eyes with me. "To love, to cherish, until death parts us."

"They are nice vows," I say.

"Did you mean them when you said them?" he asks.

"Of course I did."

"So did I. From the moment the judge said, 'I now pronounce you husband and wife,' you were mine, Callie. You don't get to just walk away. If you're worried about the baby thing, we'll deal with it. Together. Because that's what partners do. This isn't a pretend marriage or a temporary marriage. This is real and I'm in for the long haul. You with me?"

I tilt my head. "I'm scared."

He pulls me to his chest and holds me there, letting me feel what I'm feeling while I'm safely encircled in his strong arms.

"Ever since I was young, I've had this weird unsettling feeling in my chest. Like I had some sort of wild beast prowling around on the inside. That probably sounds crazy." He blows out a breath. "The Army sort of helped because it let me get out some of that restlessness, or maybe it was rage. I don't know. I don't feel like I was ever particularly angry, just unsettled. Prison certainly didn't help because it just made me feel like I'd caged the beast."

His big hand rubs my back, soothing me, all the while telling me a story about his broken parts.

"Do you know what finally helped?"

I shake my head, sitting up to look at him.

"Listening to you. Hearing your voice the first time you read to those kids at storytime soothed me in a way I'd never experienced. I couldn't explain it. But I reworked my schedule so I could be there every Thursday to hear you. I wanted to do more than just listen to you talk to other people though. I wanted your words, your attention. You settled me, just being near you. You center me and calm me and make me feel like I'm finally home."

"Roe," his name comes out in a sob.

"You want to be a mother, we'll figure out a way to have kids. No matter what it takes, or how much it costs. I'll give you anything you want, baby. You need to understand the *only* thing I want is you. I don't want a different wife or a younger wife. Just you. You're who I would pick. Every time, it's you. My heart beats only for you."

"I love you, Roe."

"I love you too, Callie. So damn much."

"I'm sorry I second guessed you."

"It's okay, Buttons. Tomorrow I'm going to get our vows tattooed down my ribs so you'll never forget."

epilogue

. . .

FIVE YEARS *later*

Monroe

I stand at the closed bedroom door listening for any remaining sounds. When I don't hear any, I pad my way downstairs. I find my gorgeous wife lying on her side, e-reader in hand.

I close the door quietly and lock it.

"Are they asleep?" she asks, looking up from her book.

"Yes, finally." I narrow my eyes are her. "Geriatric, rotten eggs, my ass."

She giggles. "How was I supposed to know we'd be so fertile together?"

That's right. After five years of marriage, we have three perfect kids. We would have had more, but because of Callie's hip, she has to have c-sections and after the last one, the doctor advised we be done.

"Might I point out that twins come from your side of the family?" she says.

Our oldest two, Amber and Avery, are like miniature versions of their mama. Sassy, little red-headed beasties with copper eyes and smiles that get them pretty much anything they want.

I crawl up the bed and pull up her night shirt, finding the words I seek imprinted across her ribs. Her vows to me are forever inked into her perfectly pale skin. It's the only tattoo she says she'll ever have.

It matches the one on my ribs. When we lay side-by-side, the words line up.

Callie rolls over, pressing me to my back, and kisses me. Her tongue slides against mine and I'm instantly hard.

"Christ woman, you're going to make me black out. My blood rushed so fast to my dick, it made me dizzy."

"You're so dramatic." She pulls down my pajama pants and my cock springs free. And then she's lowering herself down on top of me. Her slick pussy walls swallow up my shaft and fuck she feels so perfect. How can it always feel so fucking perfect?

"You look like a goddamn queen up there riding me like that," I tell her.

"I'm like Lady Godiva."

I reach up and palm her tits, pinching her nipples and she whimpers in response. She keeps fucking me, rocking and grinding her pussy down on me so she gets the pressure she needs on her clit. It won't take her long. It won't take either of us long.

"You're so damn beautiful, Callie." I love the way carrying our babies has changed her body, mapped new lines across her skin. "You will always be the most beautiful woman in the world to me."

"I love you, Roe. Oh shit, I'm gonna come."

"That's it, come all over my cock." She does, squeezing and milking me tight.

She collapses next to me and we snuggle into each other.

"Do you know how much I love you?" I ask.

She wraps her arms around me and grins up at me. "Tell me."

"I love you more than I love pie."

Her mouth widens in shock. "Even the coconut cream pie from Ruthie's diner?"

"It's true," I say with a nod. "And I love you more than books."

"Monroe Crawford, that's a lot of love," she says.

"I love you more than I've ever loved anything or anyone combined and then multiplied by infinity."

She laughs. "Now you sound like Harry."

Harry. My son. A miniature replica of me, down to the muddy colored eyes. He's always trying to come up with crazy ways to tell us how much he loves us. His most recent, "more than Aunt Rory's bunnies times seven."

Yep, my kids are adorable. My wife is beautiful. And our life is pretty much perfect. All my siblings eventually got married and had kids too.

As for what happened with our land and The Dark Lord's trust... I can't tell you everything.

lone star husband

. . .

HARRISON

Eight months ago I married a stranger to help

with a "green card" situation. Now I need a wife for real to help save my family's ranch. I've only met Birdie the one time, but I remember very clearly that she's remarkably smart, adorably shy and has curves I want to spend the rest of my life exploring. But now I have to give her an ultimatum: either be my wife for real or we have to get divorced so I can find someone else for the job. The only problem; she's the only woman I want.

Birdie

The only thing I remember about the man who came to my rescue is that he's a barrel-chested, thick-thighed, bearded cowboy who keeps invading my dreams. Okay, so I remember a lot about Harrison. But our union was for nothing more than practicality as far as he's concerned. Our union serves a practical purpose as far as he's concerned, but for me, there's more to the story. Like the fact he saved me from an unwanted arranged marriage to an obnoxious crown prince. I just want to lead an ordinary life, and now I know I want that life to be with Harrison. But will he want me if learns the truth about my past?

ten

. . .

Lone Star Husband

HARRISON

I'm the fourth of six and I'm a twin. I grew up never having anything that was just my own. To this day, I still live on the ranch that I run with two of my brothers. I love the ranch—and my brothers when they aren't being dumbasses. I'd do anything for my family but there are times when I crave solitude. Especially when I have a problem that needs solving.

Which is why I made this trip from Saddle Creek to Houston by myself. I needed time to think. Time to plan.

It's been less than two full weeks since we found out that our grandfather has some crazy shit written into his will. The old man—much like Voldemort himself—is too mean to die without a fight. Although, he's had a stroke, which means that day might not be too far off. Our asshole uncle—whom we call Uncle Umbridge—didn't want us to know any of this. Why? Because if our grandfather dies before we're married—with prenups he approves of—our land could go to Uncle Umbridge.

If it was simply a matter of finding someone to marry, I could do that. Don't get me wrong, I don't want to jump into marriage just to satisfy the requirements of my grandfather's will, but I could.

Except I can't.

Because I'm already married.

It's a long story. One I haven't shared with anyone in my family, except my brother Roe. It was Roe who suggested I skip town without telling the rest of the Crawford clan about my marriage, that I talk to Birdie first and figure out where she's at before I spill the beans to the rest of the jackals.

Don't get me wrong. I love my family. Even the ones who piss me off most of the time. But, sometimes, I need for them to not be up in my business.

I'm thankful as fuck I made the right choice in confiding my secret to Roe. It's given me a blissful twelve hours of silence. The entire drive from Saddle Creek to Houston, and my night in the hotel.

I could've tried to get in touch with Birdie last night. I have her address and her phone number. But I just needed the time by myself to figure out how the hell I'm going to handle this.

Seeing my wife after eight months is weird

because not only do I know next to nothing about her, but she's also my wife in name only.

What I do know is that she's from Saldania, which is some tiny country in the North Sea near Finland. I'd never even heard of it and had to look it up on Google Maps. Mike, my best friend growing up, was having trouble getting Birdie's work visa renewed because her parents are diplomats and had arranged a marriage for her back home.

I would've helped just because Mike asked, but finding out what I did about her situation sealed the deal. No grown-ass woman in the modern world should have her career hamstrung because her parents are trying to arrange a marriage for her. That's bullshit, no matter where you're from.

So I stepped in to help. Eight months ago, I told my brothers and sister I was visiting Mike for the weekend, drove down to Houston, and married Birdie seventeen minutes after meeting her for the first time. Less than twenty-four hours later, I was back in Saddle Creek, and I haven't seen or spoken to her since.

Now I'm sitting in my truck, parked in the multi-level parking garage near Mike's office. My phone has been vibrating with incoming messages for the last fifteen minutes. Clearly, my siblings are now all aware of why I've left town.

I open my messages to our group text that my sister annoying named, "The Jolly Ranchers."

MADISON: So are we not gonna talk about the fact that Harrison left town to go get his WIFE?

MADISON: His WIFE!!!

JOHNNY: Wait, what?

HAYES: In a meeting, so I'm muting y'all.

MADISON: <gif of the Olson twins rolling their eyes>

MADISON: Do you think he even read my original text and realizes his twin brother is married?

QUINN: Did anyone know?

ROE: He told me before he left town. Mostly because he knew y'all would ask questions.

QUINN: Obviously that's why he didn't tell Mad. She would've had 172 questions.

MADISON: As if y'all don't have them too. I mean seriously? How has he kept this from us? Where is she? How did they meet? How long have they been married?

JOHNNY: Exactly. I want to know everything too. Damn. About to

> take a test though so I'm going dark.
>
> HARRISON: I will answer y'all's questions when I get home.
>
> MADISON: OMG! Harrison? Are you with her now? What's her name? Can we have a picture?
>
> QUINN: Jesus, Mad, this is why no one talks to you.
>
> MADISON: <emoji of middle finger>
>
> HARRISON: Patience, Mad. I'll either show you a picture or you'll be meeting her soon.

With that, I silence and pocket my phone, then get out of my truck. I glance down at myself and wonder if I should've dressed up more. The truth is, I'm a simple cowboy. I married her to help her with a situation and now I need her to reciprocate. So it shouldn't matter if I'm wearing jeans and a t-shirt.

I already know that my buddy, Mike, isn't in the office because he's traveling to some gaming con.

Plus, I'm not here to see him.

I get off the elevator on the floor for PenDragon Games and find myself facing a large reception desk. As I exit the elevator, a woman nearly runs straight into me. She skitters back a step, like my very presence startled her. I'm a big motherfucker, despite my efforts to change some of that. I can't do a damn thing about my height, but I did try diets and eating salads for a while to try to slim my waistline.

Nothing worse than being one half of a set of fraternal twins and you're known as the "fat one." Hayes, my brother, he would be the "hot one." Whatever. So yeah, I'm a big guy. I'm strong as the proverbial ox and I'm thick everywhere. My oldest brother, Quinn, is sort of built the same, but he has more definition in his abs. I've got abs, they're just under a layer of padding. Or a layer of pudding as my Mama used to say.

Behind the reception desk, there's a massive wall of frosted glass with the company's name and logo etched into it. Behind the desk are two people—a guy with short-cropped bright blue hair, and a petite woman with owlish eyes.

I walk up to the desk, tip my hat, and say to the woman, "Excuse me, ma'am."

She blinks up at me, then titters. Probably because she's younger than me and I called her "ma'am." I know my manners are old-fashioned, but it's how I was raised.

"Can I help you?"

"I'm looking for—"

Before I can finish the sentence, the guy elbows his co-worker and steps up to the desk. "Oh, my God. You're Birdie's husband."

The woman looks at him, confused, then back at me.

I clear my throat, uncertain what the right response is here. I didn't tell anyone in Saddle Creek about the wedding and it didn't occur to me that she might have handled things differently on her end.

Understanding dawns on the woman's face. "You are, aren't you?"

I nod, reluctantly.

She titters again, shooting a conspiratorial grin at the guy. "We were beginning to think you weren't real." She leans in and whispers as if confiding in me. "We actually have an office pool."

"A what?"

"You know, like a bet. I mean, she has a picture of you in her office from y'all's wedding. And she talks about you, but no one has ever seen you. And you never call." She lifts a bony shoulder in a shrug. "We sorta thought you weren't real."

I stare at the woman, waiting for the punchline because surely that's not it. Do all of Birdie's colleagues whisper this shit behind her back?

"Some of us thought you were a figment of her imagination," the woman continues. "She's a strange one, that Birdie."

I don't try to hide my glare. "I think 'creative' is the word you're looking for. Or perhaps intelligent. My wife is brilliant, and as you can see, I'm not a figment of her imagination." I hold my arms out to emphasize my size.

The woman eyes me up and down and visibly swallows. "Yes, I do see. Well, she should be in her office." She scurries around the reception desk and uses a badge to swipe open the door. Gesturing me in, she adds loud enough that others can hear, "Birdie's office is the third door on the left. But since you're her husband, I'm sure you know that."

Offices line the outer rim of the floor, but the center is a weird combination of beanbag chairs, yoga balls, large pillows, and gaming chairs. Seems like everyone is wearing those giant headphones covering their ears.

I nod and walk away, but I can hear the whispers all around me. I glance back over my shoulder and see that the guy from reception has joined the woman, along with two other people, and they're all whispering.

If they hadn't been paying attention before, they sure are now. I wonder if Mike knows how much time his underlings spend gossiping.

The offices that line the bullpen all have big glass windows. So as soon as I spot Birdie's office, I can see her through the window. My steps slow as I drink in the sight of her. Her desk is angled toward the opposite wall, so she doesn't see me. Maybe I should have called or texted her to warn her I was coming.

By the time I reach her office doorway, my

stomach is tied in knots. But there she is, sitting behind her desk looking cute as fuck with a set of pink headphones with cat ears on top of two ash-blonde braids. The walls of her office are plastered in posters. Some are music bands, but others must be for video games because I don't recognize them. The space between her keyboard and the multiple monitors is taken up with dozens of tiny figurines and miniature toys. She's dressed in a vintage Atari shirt that V's deep into her lush cleavage.

Like the first time I laid eyes on my wife, I go rock hard behind my zipper. She hasn't seen me yet, so I just stand there and watch her for a minute as her eyes flick from one of the three monitors in front of her to another. She frowns, then bites down on her lip. Then she nods and reaches for the desk and picks up a partially eaten jelly donut. She takes a bite and a huge glob of red gelatinous filling falls right into her cleavage.

And that's when she looks up and sees me.

eleven

...

Lone Star Husband

BIRDIE

There comes a time in every woman's life when the sexy beast of a man from her dreams walks into her office just in time to see her drop jam filling from a pastry right into her bosom. Okay, no. That doesn't happen to *every* woman. Only me. Because I'm *that* girl.

The fact that this sexy beast of a man is my husband should make this less awkward. But since I barely know Harrison, and have spent a total of two hours in his company, it doesn't.

I met and married Harrison all in one day, eight months ago, because my manipulative parents were trying to use their status as diplomats to get me deported back to Saldania. They mean well … at least, they claim to mean well. They only want what's best for me, blah, blah, blah.

But since the last thing I want in life is to return to Saldania and the marriage they've arranged for me there, I threw myself at the mercy of Mike, my boss at PenDragon Gamer Inc. to see if he had any brilliant ideas.

A lawyer friend of Mike's suggested a marriage to a US citizen would help on multiple fronts, and Mike swore he knew a guy.

Not in the mafia sense of, "Yeah, I know a guy," but in a, "Harrison is a great guy and he'll step up, do me a solid and it won't be creepy or weird, I promise," sense.

I'm not going to pretend marrying a total stranger is the smartest, most reasonable thing I've ever done, but I was desperate. So I agreed.

I never expected I'd feel a soul-deep connection with Harrison the moment I met him. I never imagined he'd make me feel so safe and cared for. And I never anticipated spending hours gazing at the simple ring he slipped onto my finger during the ceremony, even after he returned to the small town where he lives. I printed out the single photo Mike snapped and framed it so it could sit on my desk.

And on my bedside table.

And I have a smaller one in my purse.

Yes, I know I'm ridiculous

I know my fascination with him is ill-conceived

and ill-fated. I know it will never lead to anything. I know he's my husband in name only and never agreed to anything more than that.

But a girl can dream, can't she?

Part of me thought I'd never see Harrison again. So when he shows up at work, I'm gobsmacked.

"Harrison!" I try to stand, but I'm tangled in the cord from my headset because, of course, I'm not wearing my wireless ones. I make a super ungraceful noise when my head jerks back and I fall into my chair with a thud.

He doesn't seem swayed by the train wreck of destruction that is currently me. His eyes are heated as he closes my office door and crosses the distance between us.

I'm dreaming, right? I mean, I must be. So many of my dreams have started this way—although none of them involved the pastry filling currently oozing into my bra.

"Hey, Birdie."

That deep, rumbly voice pours over me like a melted chocolate. Was he this big when we got married? And this ruggedly handsome with his cropped blond hair and trimmed beard a shade darker?

I'm about to return his greeting when he lowers his head and kisses me.

Kisses me! Why is he kissing me? Why am I not kissing him back?

Okay, remedying that last bit straight away. I part my lips and our tongues touch. Oh, Lord, I think my panties just ignited. Like, they're actually on fire. I wonder if they'll trigger the fire alarms or ceiling sprinklers?

He makes a growly noise in the back of his throat before ending our kiss.

I'm pretty sure I look like a cartoon as I chase his lips, rising on my toes to keep them on mine for as long as possible. I don't know if he'll ever kiss me again and I don't want this moment to end.

But he's right there, his heated mouth whispering in my ear. "Sorry to ambush you like this. Your co-workers are nosy and evidently thought I wasn't real. They're watching." He grabs my chin before I can turn to look out my window that overlooks the bullpen area of the office. "Had to make this look real for them."

I exhale slowly. "Right. For appearances." So that probably was our first and last kiss. "Of course."

He leans back enough so I can see his thickly-lashed hazel eyes. How is it fair that his lashes are so naturally thick and dark?

"I have jam in my bra."

His eyes drop to my cleavage and… are his pupils dilating? His lips quirk. "Yes, I saw that right before I came in. Pesky things, those jelly donuts."

Suddenly beyond nervous, I stumble back a step. I grab a tissue from the box on my desk and wipe at the smear of jam. His gaze follows the actions of my fingers and I feel my cheeks flame.

I wish—desperately—that I could be chill about … well, anything … but this in particular.

Since I can't, I cut to the chase. "What are you doing here?"

"We need to talk. Can I take you to lunch so we can have some privacy?"

I'm still reeling from his sudden kiss, and he's shifted gears like the world didn't come to a screeching halt. "Uh, sure. Let me just grab my stuff."

While I'm packing up my main laptop and the rest of my necessary equipment—because let's face it, if I'm going to leave the office now, I'm going to finish the day at my apartment—I'm acutely aware of Harrison manhandling my desk toys.

It makes me feel self-conscious. Partly because he's here in my office, a space that—despite the huge plate glass window—is my private space. But also because they're all toys. Things I fiddle or play with when I need something to occupy my hands so my brain can be busy.

When you work in gaming, lots of people have toys littered on their desks. It's as normal as the massive beanbags, yoga ball chairs, and the tower of mega Jenga blocks. But in the hands of my husband, the tiny toys seem juvenile. Like I'm the feckless child my parents always accuse me of being. The kid who refuses to grow up.

So I half expect Harrison to criticize my toys.

Instead he holds up a Rubik's Cube and marvels, "This Rubik's cube is smaller than my thumb. Are you supposed to be able to twist and solve it?"

I don't glance up because my panties do not need a reminder of how big his fingers are, but I don't hear censure in his voice. Which only makes me want to look at him. Which is not helping. It's one thing to harbor unrealistic fantasies about your fake husband when he lives five hours away, but another thing entirely to do so when he's standing in your office, handling your toys.

And you don't mean that metaphorically, but wish you did.

Yikes. I've got it bad.

"Yes, it really works. So does my Spud Bud." I indicate the dress-up potato man, trying to steer my mind back to safe topics.

Finally, I'm packed and ready to go. He takes my bag from me and loops it over one of his massive shoulders, then places his hand at the small of my back. The gesture is kind and thoughtful and sexy all at the same time.

As he guides me through the office, I concentrate on breathing deeply to keep myself from swooning.

Once we're alone in the elevator, after being

gawked at by my entire office, he glances down at me. "Where's your car?"

I shake my head. "I don't drive. Don't have a license."

He frowns. "How do you get to and from work?"

I lift a shoulder. "Public transit. Sometimes I walk."

"You walk? Alone?"

"Only when the weather is nice."

He makes a low growl-type noise at the back of his throat.

"Did you just growl at me?"

"It's not safe for you to be walking around this city alone."

My entire body warms at the thought of him worrying about my safety. Which is ridiculous. We barely know each other. Though I certainly *feel* like I know him.

Months and months of filthy dreams about someone will do that to you. I know I'm blushing but, thankfully, the darkness of the parking garage hides it. He stops at a big pickup truck and leads me around to the passenger side. His hands are on my waist and he's lifting me up before I even know what's happening.

I can feel the heat of his hands through my tee-shirt, and I want to wrap my legs around his waist and pull him toward me.

But then the moment is over and he's climbing into the driver's side.

Everything that's happened today has me shell-shocked. Okay, when I say "today," I really mean the past fifteen minutes. Honestly, I'm so unsettled by his presence, I don't know if I'll be able to sit still through a ride to a restaurant, let alone lunch itself.

Once he starts the truck, I turn toward him. "You don't have to take me to lunch. We can just talk here, or you can take me home."

He blows out a breath and then faces me. "I don't even know where to start with this."

My stomach knots, but I do my best to keep my worry off my face. He wants a divorce. That's what's happening. He's met someone. A woman he can love and be with and he wants to ditch me. And who could blame him? So far, Anthony hasn't found me, so who's to say he'll miraculously find me once my marriage to Harrison is over?

I brace myself for whatever he's about to say. "Just tell me."

He rubs a hand down the front of his shirt and while I'm sure he doesn't mean the movement to be sensual and tempting, it totally is. He's so big and thick and I want to crawl into his lap and snuggle into his strength and warmth. Let his belly cushion me and his bulging arms protect me.

"There's a weird clause in my grandfather's trust that puts my family's ranch in danger. In order for us to keep everything in our names, we have to marry with a prenuptial agreement. Basically, our grandfather is a giant ass and doesn't want any outsiders, even our own children, getting their hands on any of his assets." He rolls his eyes.

I'm trying to follow where he's leading me, but I'm confused.

"In our case, it would need to be a postnup since we're already married. Unless you don't want to stay married, in which case, we need to dissolve this union so I can find another wife." He blows out another breath as he finishes talking.

"What exactly do you need me to do? Just sign some paperwork?"

"Well, yes, but there's more to it than that. My uncle is a—" he clears his throat as if cutting off a slur. "Most likely, he'll try to fight this. Try to prove our marriage isn't real. So I need you to move back to Saddle Creek with me and live as my wife. For at least a year, possibly longer."

Live together. As husband and wife.

"Oh," I murmur. I sit back against the seat, my mind reeling.

As husband and wife? What does that mean? That he wants to touch me? I lick my lips and his eyes darken as they drop to my mouth. I think back to our kiss in my office. Not technically our first, but definitely our first with tongue.

If he wants us to live together as husband and

wife, maybe it won't be our only kiss. The thought of him putting those big, beefy hands on my body has me so aroused it's a wonder he can't scent it on me. He may remind me of the hot bear-shifters I read about, but he's not an actual shape-shifter. He doesn't have a heightened animalistic sense of smell.

"Birdie?" he asks.

"Yes, I'll sleep with you." I squeeze my eyes shut as I hear the words out loud. "I mean, I'll come back and sleep in your house or whatever. Be your wife." I give him a weak laugh. "Sometimes the American idioms still confuse me."

He gives me a strange look, but nods. "Excellent. Let's go pack your things."

twelve

Lone Star Husband

HARRISON

By the time we get Birdie packed up and drive back to Saddle Creek, it's well past dark. She falls asleep about an hour into the journey, but the bumpiness of the long gravel drive leading to the ranch house wakes her.

"We're here," I say, putting my truck in park. I'm thankful I don't see any of my other siblings vehicles except for Quinn's.

I go around and help Birdie down and then lead her to the front of the house.

"How can you see anything out here?" she asks.

I chuckle. "I'm used to it, growing up out here." I look down at her blonde head, her braids tousled from her nap in my truck. "Does your country not have parts where you're away from city lights and it gets so dark you see all the stars?"

She glances up and gasps. "Not like this. At least, not that I remember."

She hasn't told me much about where she's from, but I know it's an island nation somewhere in the North Sea.

The front door opens, and Quinn appears. "Hey, brother. Need some help?"

"There are bags and a few boxes in the back of the truck. I'm going to show Birdie to Madison's old room, I think she'll be more comfortable in there."

Quinn shakes his head. "No can do. I hired a live in housekeeper. Name's Amber and that's where she's staying."

"Where's Birdie supposed to—?"

"She's your wife, Harrison. I'm sure you'll figure it out." He stops in front of Birdie and holds out his hand. "I'm Quinn, the oldest of the crew."

"Birdie."

The warm smile she gives him pisses me off. I wrap my arm around her and curve my fingers around her waist, pulling her closer to me. "Come on, Birdie, I'll show you my room. You can get settled while Quinn and I carry your stuff in."

"Nice to meet you," she tells me my brother.

I lead her away and up the stairs to my bedroom. I try to remember if I made my bed before I left town, but at this point it doesn't really matter. It's a single bedroom in my late parent's house. We own enough property to build other houses on the ranch, which is what my parents always dreamed of for us, but until we get this trust crap resolved, it's not happening.

"So this is my room. Well, our room, I guess. Sorry about us having to share a bed."

She frowns at me. "I actually assumed when you asked me to come live with you as your wife, that we would be sleeping together." She bites down on her lip. "Sharing a room."

Sleeping together.

The words coming out of Birdie's mouth conjure all kinds of filthy images. All of them involve her naked and riding my dick.

I scrub a hand down my face. "Right. Well, bathroom is through that door. Help yourself to whatever. I'll go get the rest of your stuff."

Then like a chicken shit, I turn and leave the room. Fuck, she's too much of a temptation, especially now I've had a taste of the sweetness that is her mouth.

I meet Quinn outside and immediately jump into helping unload Birdie's things. He's got a bunch of it already piled on the porch.

"Doesn't sound like she's from around here," Quinn observes.

"She's not."

Quinn eyes me but doesn't inquire further. "Bluebonnet festival tomorrow."

"Fuck, forgot about that."

Quinn nods. "There's a chance Uncle Umbridge will be in town for it."

I stop and stare at my oldest brother. "Why?"

"He heard about Roe's marriage. I'm guessing he's come to check in. He'll be watching you closely now you've brought a *wife* home."

"Can you quit saying *wife* like she's some kind of alien?"

Quinn shoots a glare at me. "Eight fucking months, Harrison, and you didn't think to tell any of us?"

"It wasn't supposed to matter."

"Well, whatever she is to you, you better put on a fucking show tomorrow because he'll be watching."

We carry the rest of her stuff inside.

"We can get this upstairs tomorrow. I'm fucking tired from all the driving," I say.

Quinn nods. "Hayes says he's coming in too."

My heart tightens. My twin and I haven't been close in a long time so it shouldn't hurt that he told Quinn instead of me about him coming into town. Still, I can't deny the twinge of pain that jets through me at the news.

"Who's the new housekeeper?" I ask, changing the subject.

"Her name is Amber. She's from out of town."

I frown. "Does she have experience?"

Quinn lifts a shoulder in a shrug. "She's young.

But she made breakfast this morning and it was good. Cleaned the whole house too. I figure she'll learn as she goes."

"Am I missing something?"

"She was in a bad situation. I got her out. Now she's safe. That's all you need to know."

"If you say so." I rub the back of my neck and eye the staircase. "Guess I better get to bed."

"Your wife is waiting for you."

It's on my tongue to tell him to fuck off, but he's just stating the obvious. Birdie *is* my wife. And she is upstairs in my bed. Just that thought has my cock stirring behind my zipper.

I turn away from my brother and head up the stairs. "Thanks for the help."

By the time I make it up the stairs I've convinced myself that sharing a bed with Birdie is not a big deal. I'm a twin, and I have three other brothers and a sister. I shared a damn bed for more than half my life. I can do this.

I go through the motions in the bathroom, getting myself ready for bed. Birdie is quiet and under the covers by the time I come into my darkened bedroom. She's on the pillow I normally sleep on, but I find I don't mind at all. I lift the blankets to crawl in next to her, thankful that the bed is at least a queen.

Then I see her curvy ass, encased in black cotton panties decorated with little gaming controllers on them in bright neon colors. Her shirt is pulled up, baring a swath of creamy, pale skin at her lower back. Her legs are bare, and I want to crawl between those thick thighs and bury my face in her pussy. Lick her awake. Discover her sweet, musky taste and the sound she makes when she cries my name in climax.

I'm a fucking idiot. This is way different than sharing a bed with one of my siblings as a kid. I climb in and face away from her tempting curves. I'm so close to the edge of the bed, it'll be a miracle if I don't fall out before morning.

thirteen

Lone Star Husband

BIRDIE

Sometime in the middle of the night, I wake, and I'm not sure if I'm pressed to Harrison's body or he's pressed to mine. All I know is that our limbs are entangled, our fingers are entwined, and the warmth of his breath next to me on the pillow makes me smile.

Maybe there's some hope for us to become a real couple. I know it won't take much for me to fall completely in love with this man I married.

But when I wake in the morning, I'm alone in our bed. The sun shines through the window to my right, and the spot where Harrison's body was feels cool. He's been out of bed for a while.

I glance at the clock on the nightstand and note that it's already well after nine. I never sleep this late. But if I'm honest with myself, I haven't slept that soundly in a long time. Maybe ever.

I quickly shower and braid my hair before dressing and making my way downstairs. I find a woman in the living room vacuuming, and she screams when I step into the room.

"Oh, my Lord, you scared me half to death. You must be Harrison's wife." Her Texas twang is thick, and she smiles at me.

"I am. My name is Birdie."

Her eyes widen. "Oh, your accent is so pretty. Are you from England or something?"

I nod. "Something like that." I'm not trying to be evasive, but Saldania is so tiny, most people have never heard of it, so I'm used to glossing over the details to save time. I glance around the house. "Do you know where Harrison is?"

"Oh, well, all the guys are out working. They start early here on the ranch. I'm new here too. I'm Amber, by the way. Quinn hired me as the new housekeeper."

"Wow, you seem kind of young to be a housekeeper."

She lifts a shoulder. "It's work I enjoy. And I'm a good cook. Made homemade biscuits this morning. There's still some in the kitchen if you want some."

"That sounds lovely. American biscuits, I'm assuming? Not what you would call cookies?"

"Correct. I can make you some cookies if you'd prefer."

I shake my head. "No, biscuits sound good." Honestly, in the time I've lived in the U.S, I've become obsessed with southern buttermilk biscuits.

I follow Amber into the kitchen and she sets me up with a plate of biscuits and butter. We chat for a while as I eat my breakfast, then I head upstairs to try to figure out my new life. At least, for the time being. As I step into our bedroom, I see that Harrison moved most of my stuff in this morning and, somehow, I slept through it. There's a note taped to one of the boxes. My heart skitters as I pick it up.

Birdie,
Make yourself at home. We have a town festival we need to attend tonight. It's casual and outdoors so don't worry about dressing fancy. See you around four.
Harrison.

There's nothing romantic about his note. Obviously. Why am I looking for romance? I shake my head to try to clear my thoughts. Evidently, our kiss yesterday rattled me in more ways than one.

According to Harrison, the Bluebonnet Festival happens every year in late March in Saddle Creek. I assumed it would be in the town square, but it's on a wildflower farm a few miles outside of town.

And, yes, a wildflower farm is exactly what it

sounds like. Field upon field of wildflowers. There's a visitor's center wedged between a bluebonnet field, and a field of dark orange Indian Paintbrushes. At one end, there's a stage where live music is playing, and food trucks and craft vendors along the other.

I've met most of Harrison's siblings so far, except his twin who, thus far, is a no-show. But the rest have all been friendly and welcoming. I like Roe's wife, Callie, who is the town librarian. Her best friend, Rory, is hilarious, telling stories about her small farm animals she brought around for kids' birthday parties and whatnot. She has some here at the festival set up as a little petting zoo.

My father bought me an entire stable full of ponies one year for my birthday, despite the fact I was terrified of the creatures. I tried to go out to the pastel-painted barn, but the first pony I attempted to pet had nipped at me. I screamed and cried and hid in my room for three days until my father sold the entire collection.

Harrison has disappeared, promising to return to my side soon and leaving me with his sister, Madison. I like Madison, although I find her slightly intimidating.

She scoots her chair closer to mine. "I figure now is as good a time as any to give you the dirt on the rest of the family."

"The dirt?"

"You know, the gossip or the low-down. All the

good stuff." She gives me a big smile. "I adore your accent, which I'm sure you hear all the time."

"When I talk, yes, but I often work alone so I don't speak to people too much."

"So where exactly are you from?"

"It's a small island nation between Great Britain and Finland. It's called Saldania."

"That's so cool. How the hell did you even end up in Texas?"

I lift a shoulder. "Video games. They're not very big back home, and our society is still old-ashioned so it would have been difficult for me to get a job in the field. Here, I get to write and design the games I love to play."

"Wow. That's amazing. And brave of you to leave your home. Do you miss your family?"

"Yes, I suppose. But my parents aren't—" I pause, mulling over my words. I don't want to say the wrong thing here, especially since it's obvious the Crawfords are very close, "—affectionate. I mean, I love them. Obviously. And they love me," I say quickly, seeing Madison's frown. "But they were gone a lot when I was kid. Traveling for work."

"What kind of work? I thought you said it was small country."

"Mostly they came to the US. They were diplomats, so I attended high school in New York. Staying here for university made sense, and then …" I let my words trail off, hoping she won't ask more questions about them.

"And here I've been living in this same town pretty much my whole life. Still, I got my business associates degree to help run my store downtown."

"Did you ever want to go anywhere else?" I ask her.

"When I was young, I wanted to. I thought I needed to go away to meet my prince charming." Madison releases a humorless laugh. "Then I met him right here in Saddle Creek."

"I didn't realize you were in a relationship."

"I'm not. He changed his mind about us. Right before we said our vows. I'm surprised you haven't heard the story. People here love to talk about Madison, the jilted bride."

"Oh, how dreadful. That must have been terrible."

"It was. But it's been a few years now. And he better not show his face around here again or my brothers will line up to kick his ass."

"I imagine they would."

Madison waves her hand in the air as if to erase it. "Let's move on from all that junk. How about I get back to that family dirt I was going to share. First, I have to know about this new live-in housekeeper Quinn hired. Have you met her?" she asks, her eyes practically glowing with curiosity.

"Amber? Yes, I met her this morning. She's very sweet."

"Pretty?"

"Yes. She seems quite young, though."

Madison's brows go up. "Interesting. Okay, so here's what you need to know about our crew. Quinn, he's the eldest. He's also the bossiest and surliest."

That makes me smile. I only met Quinn briefly, but her description seems to fit.

Madison nods to the table to our left. "Roe is the next eldest. I'm sure you've heard the rumors about how he recently got out of prison. He's not scary, though, so don't worry. And if you have questions, just ask. He's always been on the quiet side and restless, but since he married Callie, he's all smiles. It's like she settles him. They're good for each other."

"They're adorable together," I say. It's hard to not feel a pinch of envy, though I have no right. They met and fell in love

"Johnny Crawford, I swear on all that is holy, if you don't put me down, I will shave your head," a girl yells as the youngest Crawford runs past with the girl hanging over his broad shoulder.

He just laughs uproariously as he goes.

Madison rolls her eyes. "Johnny is obviously the youngest, and as you can see, he gets away with just about anything."

"Is that his girlfriend?" I ask.

"No. That's his best friend, Harper. They've been friends since grade school. They're always like that. In any case, he's spoiled rotten, but sweet as pie and everyone loves him."

We stare at the stage as the band comes back from their break and begins to warm up.

"As you can tell, I'm the know it all, mother hen of the group," she says.

"The only girl?"

She nods. "Yep, the only girl.

"What about Hayes? I haven't met him yet."

"Yeah, he was supposed to be here tonight, but he probably had a very important business meeting." Madison rolls her eyes. "He and Harrison couldn't be more different, even when they were kids. Hayes was always the charmer. They look nothing alike and, frankly, don't even act like brothers. Hayes got out of Saddle Creek as soon as he graduated high school. I don't think he'll ever come back."

fourteen

...

Lone Star

HARRISON

I hate leaving Birdie alone at the festival, but I already agreed to do a short set with the band. My sister assured me she'd take good care of my wife in my absence. But Madison isn't who I'd be worried about, anyways.

Birdie looks so damn pretty tonight, with her long blonde hair in those twin braids she's so fond of. The jeans she's wearing hug her plump curves and round ass. I had to stop myself from grabbing hold of her bottom several times when we were walking to the square from my truck. Her pink t-shirt is fitted tight across her full tits, and there's some animated cat dancing across her boobs. I might have recognized the critter, but the more I looked, the more I felt like I was staring at her nipples so I forced my gaze away.

Staring into her chocolate brown eyes isn't any safer, though. Frankly, there's nothing and nowhere I can look at Birdie without thinking about all the ways I want to touch her.

Christ, waking up this morning with our bodies tangled together was simultaneously the best and worst. We're married so, technically, I could pursue a physical relationship with her, but until I know where we stand, I'm not sure if she's ready for my intense my physical appetite. I want to pull her hair and fuck her six ways to Sunday, fill her belly with my seed and make sure she's carrying my kid by the end of the month. It's safe to say that being in the same bed with Birdie for only one night has made me lose my fucking mind.

I'm halfway to the stage when I spot him. My brother. My twin. I take a few steps to the side so I'm right in his line of sight. He nods and gives me that grin of his, the one that always got him whatever he wanted. First, from our Mama, and then the teachers and every other woman he's come in contact with. Even wearing jeans and a button-down shirt, he looks out of place here. He's too polished, too put together. He probably spends more on his haircuts than I do on new clothes.

When he gets close enough, he gives me one of those one-armed hugs. "It's been a while."

"Last I checked, Saddle Creek is still in the same place it's always been. Even makes it onto some maps these days."

Hayes whistles through his teeth. "Fair enough." He turns and follows my line of sight. "Oh, is that the wifey? The one sitting with Mad?"

I grunt in response. I don't want him talking about Birdie. And I sure as fuck don't want him looking at her.

"Nice, brother. She's pretty hot in a geek-girl kind of way."

"Fuck you, Hayes. Could you at least try not to be a dick about everything?"

"Dude, if your wife just moved in with you, and you're getting laid on the regular, shouldn't you be in a better mood?

I tighten my hands into fists at my sides. "Christ, Hayes. Stop talking before I punch you in the fucking teeth."

Hayes searches my face and gives me a shit-eating grin. "Wait. Are you *not* sleeping with her? Is that the problem?"

I blow out a slow breath. It won't do me any good to rise to his baiting. "I know how hard it is for you to behave like a civil human being, but can you just fucking try?"

Hayes barks out a laugh. "Yeah, sounds like you know a thing or two about being hard."

"Harrison, they're ready for you on stage," a voice to my right says.

"Yeah, you don't want to keep your fans waiting, brother. Don't worry. I'll go keep your wife company."

I lean forward and grab Hayes's shirt. "Don't you fucking touch my wife."

fifteen

Lone Star
Husband

BIRDIE

"We're going to invite up one of Saddle Creek's own to do a few songs with us," the woman at the mic says.

The crowd cheers and I clap along with them despite not knowing anyone around me.

"As you know," Madison continues, "Harrison is all about fading into the background. No fuss, no drama, no attention. Unless he's got a guitar in his hands." She nods towards the stage.

I look up and my heart falls to my toes when I see Harrison—my husband—standing at the mic. He's dressed as he was when we got here. Same dark plaid shirt, jeans, and cowboy hat sitting low on his head.

"I take it from your expression that you didn't know," Madison says.

I shake my head. "He never said anything."

"And he's never sung to you?"

"Never." But why would he? I'm no one to him. Not really.

The music starts, and I know immediately it's a popular country waltz played on the radio. I've only lived in Texas a couple of years, but I've been a fan of country music for a while.

And then he opens his mouth, and the crowd goes crazy. Women screaming, and I get it. I understand the appeal even without the singing because I think Harrison is the sexiest man I've ever met. I can't believe how much he sounds like Chris Stapleton up there with that bluesy growl.

My entire body is covered in gooseflesh and my nipples are tight points poking at the fabric of my shirt.

"Does he know?"

"Know what?" Madison asks.

"How good he is?"

She shakes her head. "No. If he knew, he'd be up there singing his own songs. I know he writes them. But he only ever does covers."

The guitar solo comes, and he's just as gifted at picking as he is as singing. I can't tell his sister this, but I'm so turned on right now, it's embarrassing. I swear he's looking at me, but with the way his hat sits, there's no way for me to tell.

The song ends and the crowd goes crazy, cheering and screaming his name.

Harrison. Harrison. Harrison.

Then they start up another. And he sings the hell out of this one too. I know I'm grinning like a fool, and by the time he's done singing the third song, I'm so in love with this man, I should be president of his fan club, not his temporary wife.

Harrison leaves the stage and I'm ready for him to come get me so we can go home, and I can persuade him to consummate our marriage. Surely that makes things like postnups and trusts more binding?

"I don't think I've ever seen you around here, pretty girl," the smooth deep voice comes from next to me.

I look up at the most handsome man I've ever seen. His bone structure is perfect and his brown hair is echoed in the honey color of his eyes. He's nothing short of beautiful.

He winks and let's those honeyed eyes travel the length of me. "Why don't you tell me your name?"

"Do these lines usually work for you? I mean, I get it. You're very pretty, in a slick, calendar, Brad Pitt, sort of way. But I'll have you know, I'm a happily married woman." I flip him off with my wedding ring finger, flashing my wedding band.

"Oh, come on, sugar," he says, reaching over to tuck a strand of my hair behind my ear.

I lose it. I grab his hand, and muscle memory kicks in. I do some kind of crazy ninja move I don't even remember learning, and then he's on his back at my feet, wincing and cradling his hand.

"What the hell, Hayes?" Madison demands.

"That's Hayes? Harrison's brother?" I ask in shock.

Madison nods.

I kick the downed brother. "You should be ashamed of yourself!"

"Birdie!" Harrison calls my name from behind me. "You okay?"

I nod. I'm breathing fast as I stare up at him. He spares a brief glance at his twin still laying on the ground. Johnny has come around to help, and Quinn is glaring at the whole display.

"Honestly, Hayes, what the hell were you thinking?" Johnny asks. "You don't flirt with your brother's wife."

"It was a joke," Hayes wheezes. "Besides, he wasn't anywhere near her. Just left her out in the crowd alone."

Harrison takes a step forward and Quinn shakes his head. "Not here, brother. Get Birdie out of here."

Harrison threads our fingers together and leads me away from the crowd. We walk for a while until we're away from the vendors and booths. Finally, he stops when we're in a darkened spot between two barn-like structures. The sounds of the festival are muted from here.

He situates me so I'm pressed up against the old wood and he's staring down at me.

"I don't want to talk about your brother," I say.

"That's too bad." His eyes search my face. "Because you taking him down like that was the single hottest thing I've ever seen."

I swallow hard. "Couldn't have been hotter than you singing."

His eyes raise to my face. "Did my singing turn you on, Birdie?"

I nod. "Harrison?"

"Yeah?"

"I'm your wife, right?"

He nods.

"Which means I can kiss you when I want, right?"

I see the surprise on his face right before I grab his shirt and pull him down for a kiss. I'm tired of waiting for life to happen to me. I want this man and I'm going for it.

He doesn't disappoint me. His lips part and our tongues meet in the middle, sliding obscenely against one another. We kiss until we're both panting.

He pulls back slightly, pressing our foreheads together. "Did my singing make you wet, my wife?"

"Yes, so wet."

"Fuck."

"Yes, please fuck me."

"Not here. But I am going to mark you because you're mine. Say it, Birdie."

"I'm yours."

Before I realize what's happened, he's got my jeans unfastened and loosened so they're pulled down to the middle of my ass. His big hand slides into the front of my panties, and I should be embarrassed by how wet he'll find me, but I'm not. I'm too aroused.

"Whose pussy is this?" he asks as one thick finger slides through my slick folds.

"It's yours, Harrison. It's your pussy."

He leans back a little to unzip his own jeans and then he's pulling out his long, hard cock. It's big and thick and, God, I want him to put it inside me.

"Spread your legs, wife."

I do as he instructs and then he's rubbing that fat cock head right over my clit. Sliding it against my needy nub, again and again.

I grip his shoulders. "Oh, God, Harrison, that feels so good. More please."

"You a greedy girl for my cock?"

"Yes, give it to me, please. Put it inside me."

"You're going to get it inside you soon. But right now, I'm going to make you come. I'm going to fill these panties with my seed so you can walk back to my truck knowing who you belong to. Then when we get home, I'm going to fuck you. That what you want, Birdie?"

"Yes. Oh, God, I'm so close. Please." I dig my nails into his shoulders and rock my pelvis against him to increase the friction of him dry rubbing my clit. But two more pumps and I shatter all over him.

"Fuck," he growls.

I feel his release, sticky, and warm shoot over my pussy and into my panties. He grips my face and kisses me hard. Lips, teeth, and tongue. I feel claimed and, somehow, freed at the same time.

sixteen

. . .

Lone Star Husband

HARRISON

I just came all over her pussy and my dick isn't even going soft. This woman has wrecked me.

"Take me home, Harrison," she says, her accent lilting her vowels. "Make me your wife in every way."

I do my best to stuff my still-hard cock back into my boxers and zip up my jeans. Then I zip up hers before grabbing her hand and pulling her out of the field to head to my truck.

Once we hit the more well-lit areas, we start to run into other people walking around. Plenty of them speak to me, mentioning my singing, as they always do. Birdie beams up at me as if she's so proud to be here, on my arm.

One thing becomes clear—I could love this woman. Hell, I think I already do. Yeah, we've been married for eight months. And yeah, we haven't seen each other in that time, but it doesn't mean I haven't done things to get to know her.

I've spent eight months following all of her social media. I've bought and learned to play every single game she's ever designed. I've watched movies she's recommended and books she's read. I've been a true and proper stalker. I know she loves eighties and nineties science-fiction movies. And that she has a slight addiction to bear-shifter romance which, in all honesty, is pretty easy to get addicted to. There's something so compelling about the notion of fated mates.

"What did my brother say to you?" I finally ask once we're alone inside the cab of my truck.

She rolls her eyes. "He's a pretty boy accustomed to getting attention. I wasn't interested."

"He knew who you were."

Her mouth opens and a 'V' forms between her brows. "And he still came on to me? What a scoundrel."

"He was trying to get to me." I shake my head as I cup her cheek. "It's obvious you've got some kickass skills, but I want you to know that I will always take care of you. And no matter what Hayes actually said, he's harmless."

"You and he are nothing alike."

"Yes, I heard plenty of that growing up."

She laughs.

I start the truck and drive.

"It's a wonder he still behaves that way. Surely he learned when the two of you were children that your way is much more pleasant and appropriate." She bites down on her lip. "Except in dark places when your mouth gets a bit wicked."

"Do I need to apologize?" I ask.

"No. I liked it. Probably too much. It was very arousing, all the things you said."

"Good. I'm going to say one more thing about my brother, then I only want to talk about us."

"Alright."

"Hayes has always been the charming one, the hot one, the preferred one. He was the twin everyone wanted. Not me."

"Well, you're the twin I want. The only man I want," she says, her voice breathless.

"Fuck, I like to hear you say that."

"How much further until we're home?"

"Is something wrong?"

"I'm just aching, and I need you."

"Goddammit, Birdie, you're fucking perfect. Do you know that?"

She laughs. "No, but I'm glad you think so. Since it's more or less dark in here, can I make a confession?"

"You can tell me anything, baby."

"Ever since our wedding, I've been fantasizing about you. I've followed you on social media, and while you don't post enough pictures of yourself, your sister posts some every now and then. I should probably thank her for that. Because they've been my fodder for my nighttime fantasies all these months."

I'm so fucking hard right now it'll be a miracle if my zipper doesn't permanently imprint on my shaft. "Tell me," I croak.

"Tell you what?"

"What did you do at night when you thought about me?"

"I thought about your big hands touching me. I thought about your gorgeous face looking down at me while you're pounding inside of me. I thought about crawling across your lap and straddling you and then riding you until we were both breathless."

"What did you do to yourself while you imagined those things?"

"I played with my pussy," she says quietly. "I'd get sopping wet. And I'd try to put a few fingers inside me, but I knew it wasn't enough. I knew nothing I could do would get me as full as you would."

"Because you knew I'd have a big fucking dick?"

"Yes. Your fingers are so thick. There's no way your cock wouldn't be even bigger."

"If we weren't about to turn down our driveway,

I'd pull this truck over and let you ride me right here. Are you on the pill or anything?"

It takes her a while to answer. "No. I haven't been sexually active, and it hasn't been necessary."

I wait until I put the truck in park before turning to face her. "Good." I climb out and walk around to help Birdie down.

"Good? What does that mean?" she asks when I pull her out of the truck.

I carry her, bridal style, to the front door of the house. Thankfully no one else is here. "It means that if I plant a baby in your belly, it will give you more reason to stay by my side as my wife."

"Do you mean that?"

"Fuck, yeah. Birdie, I want you."

"Take me, Harrison. Please take me."

She doesn't have to ask me twice. This time I carry her up the stairs to our bedroom and kick the door shut behind us.

"Get naked," I tell her. "I'm going to try to go as slow as possible, but even with what we did in town, I'm so goddamn hard right now, I could hammer nails with my cock."

She smiles widely at me as she whips off her shirt. "There's an image."

"You have no idea how much I wanted to lick that jelly out of your cleavage yesterday. We might need to re-enact the whole jelly donut debacle sometime."

She reaches behind her and undoes her bra, then

lets it slide off her shoulders onto the floor. Her tits are full and heavy with pale pink nipples that are begging for my mouth.

I take off my shirt and walk toward her, bending to swirl my tongue around a nipple. I toe off my boots while I suck and nibble on her breasts. She tries to get her jeans undone while moaning my name, but she's too distracted.

I press her tits together. "I want to fuck these beauties sometime."

"You can."

"Will you let me know if there's anything you want me to do or you want to do to me?"

She bites down on her lip.

"You already have something in mind. Spill it, baby."

"I want to sit on your face. Not now because I'm a mess down there, but maybe after a shower sometime."

"Whenever you want it, you just climb on. Consider this beard your throne."

She throws her arms around my neck and kisses all over my face and finally my lips. While we kiss, I remove the rest of her clothes, then I take a step back and finish undressing.

Her eyes are greedy as she eats up my torso. "I love how big and thick you are. So strong. Like you could shield me from anything."

I want to promise to slay all her dragons, but I'm

no prince.

She runs her hand over my chest and my stomach. "I love the hair too. It's just enough. You're so masculine."

It's on my tongue to ask her if the man she was supposed to marry in her home country isn't particularly masculine, but he has no place here in our bedroom.

I shove my jeans down and kick them and my boxers off. When I stand upright, my cock aims right at her.

Her brown eyes widen, and she licks her lips. She doesn't hesitate to wrap her fingers around my shaft. They don't quite fit all the way around, but she gives me a firm tug all the same.

"Birdie," I moan. "You don't know how long I've wanted your hands on me."

"As long as I've wanted to touch you, I hope," she whispers.

"We were two strangers that day in the courthouse."

"Didn't mean I didn't fall for you." She walks backward to the bed and tugs gently as if leading me by my dick.

"I have a confession," I say.

She falls back on the bed, her thighs parting. Her pink, slick folds peek at me between her trimmed pubic hair. She cups her tits and flicks her nipples.

"Goddamn, you're sexy."

"What's your confession?" she asks.

"I read those books you recommended on your social media. I got hooked."

She gives me a curious smile. "Which books?"

I crawl up her body, licking up her thighs, then circling her belly button with my tongue. I look up at her face. "Those bear shifter books. They're really good."

She grabs my face and pulls me up to her. Her thighs open even wider and my hips drop into the cradle of her body, nestling my erection against her hot, wet core.

"You remind me of the heroes. I think that's why I got addicted to them. It was after we met. And they're all so big and burly and fiercely protective and it worked well with my fantasies of you."

"You want me to be fiercely protective of you?" I grab her hands and hold them down on either side of her face. Then I rock my dick against her.

She hisses. "Yes. I want you to growl at other men if they look at me. I want you to glare at them and say *MINE* all possessive like. I want you to claim me."

"You want me to claim this pussy?"

"Yes, please, Harrison."

I lean back and sit on my haunches and swipe a thumb through her folds. "I need to make you come again, baby. I'm not small and I want you nice and wet so I don't hurt you."

She nods.

"Open these gorgeous thighs for me, Birdie. I love all your delicious curves." She spreads open for me. "That's it. Now pull your knees up and hold them for me."

This spreads her pussy lips wide open for me and I see her glossy desire mixed with my spend from earlier. My dick throbs, reminding me he wants inside. But he needs to wait.

I tease my finger at her entrance, just making light circles until I finally push forward. She's so damn tight it'll be a miracle if I don't come on the first thrust inside. I curve my finger up and find that spot at the front of her pussy.

Her eyes widen and she gasps when I first brush against it. "Holy wow."

"You like that?"

"Yes, yes, I do."

I add another finger, curving them both, and start my rhythm. I use the thumb of my free hand to gently rub at the hood of her clit.

"Harrison," she moans.

I keep everything steady, not increasing pressure or speed, just maintaining my touch.

"Oh, oh, oh." She shakes her head back and forth as if she's disagreeing with me, but I can feel the walls of her pussy start to flutter. Her little clit is getting tighter and firmer too. She's close.

"Just let go, Birdie. I've got you, baby. This is my pussy and I know just how to take care of her."

That's all it takes for her orgasm explodes around my hands. Her pussy convulses, fluids pulse at my fingers, and my wife shrieks my name.

I move my hands and then shift my body so I'm covering her. I line up my dick, then thrust inside her in one swift movement. Her pussy walls are still fluttering from the end of her last orgasm.

"My pussy," I say. Then I kiss her.

She kisses me back and wraps her legs around my waist. At the moment, I'll never want another woman. She's it for me. My wife. My heart. The love of my life. I want to tell her, but it's too soon, so I keep kissing her as I draw my hips back and pump inside her again.

Her nails score at my back as I fuck her, and we break free from the kiss, each of us moaning.

"You feel so goddamn perfect, Birdie."

"It's so good. Oh, my God, I never knew."

I shift my body to angle my thrusts in a way I hope aims my dick right at her G-spot. Judging by her moans, I hit it right on.

"I think I might climax again."

"Do it, baby. You come on this dick as many times as you want. Next time I might last longer. But fuck me, you're squeezing me so good."

"That's it, Harrison. Yes, I'm coming!"

Her head tilts back on the pillow and her pussy

chokes my cock sending me over the edge with her. The image of me coating the walls of her womb with my seed makes me come even harder.

I can't help but think that if I get her pregnant, I can tie her to me forever.

seventeen

Lone Star Husband

BIRDIE

I wake up with a delicious ache between my thighs. A deep rumble sounds around me and then a flash lights up the room. I glance at the window and see the rain splattering against the glass. Harrison isn't in bed, and a glance at the clock tells me why.

Even when it's raining, ranchers still get up early. I ready myself as quickly as possible, then wander downstairs. I hear the voices and laughter before I reach the first floor, and head in the direction of the kitchen where I find all the Crawford siblings sitting around the old rectangle farm table.

Amber is at the stove cooking what smells like eggs. Callie, Roe's wife, is snuggled up next to him. And I see Johnny's best friend from last night. At least

I'm assuming that's who it is. Last night I just saw her bottom when he ran past carrying her upside down.

"Good morning," I say.

"Morning, baby," Harrison replies, coming toward me. "You want some coffee or something."

"Coffee would be splendid, actually."

"Splendid," Madison says, attempting to copy my accent.

Her brothers give her crap for her poor attempt.

Then Hayes in front of me, holding his hand out. "I owe you an apology, Birdie. I was an ass last night. I shouldn't have put you in the middle of me giving Harrison shit."

I realize he has one hell of a black eye. "Oh, my God, did I do that?" I point at his shiner.

He chuckles. "No, but you could have. You should see the bruise on my back. This is from Johnny."

The youngest Crawford stands slightly and does a little bow. "Thank you, thank you."

Harrison pulls me over to the table. My stomach feels like a mess of nerves, but the thought of belonging to this family makes me smile. They give each other crap, but they also support one another. That must be so amazing.

"Madison, why don't you tell us about your walking while intoxicated citation you got last night?" Johnny quips.

"Ugh, that sheriff is a pain in my ass." Madison winces and tilts her head at Callie. "No offense to you, of course."

"None taken. My brother is obnoxious sometimes. Did he really give you a ticket?" Callie asks.

"No. But he did insist on walking me home. For my safety," Madison says in a mocking voice. "And he said it was a formal warning." She rolls her eyes. "I wasn't even drunk. I just stumbled a little while walking. Whatever."

"Mad, you've always been a lightweight. Nothing to be ashamed of. I'm glad the sheriff saw you safely home," Roe says.

"Oh, best friends with your enforcement in-law now?" Madison asks.

"If the rain ever stops, I need to go see about getting some extra insulation for Harrison's bedroom," Quinn says.

Harrison frowns. "Why do I need extra insulation? He turns to me. Were you cold last night?"

"No, I was fine."

"Might help block out some of the sound," Quinn clarifies.

I feel the blush creep up my neck and heat my cheeks. "Oh, my God. Just kill me now."

Harrison squeezes me to him and kisses my head. "Nah, baby. He's just jealous because he doesn't have a wife to call out his name like that."

"Eww, y'all are gross. No sex stories at the breakfast table," Madison says.

"Oh shit. Is that what they were talking about?" Johnny asks.

"You're adorable," his friend says on a giggle. Then she stands. She holds her hand out to me. "Sorry to meet you and run, Birdie. I'm Harper, and I've got to get into town to work. Ice cream isn't going to scoop itself. Believe me, I've tried."

Johnny stands too. "I'll drive you." He leaves the kitchen, then he comes back and pokes his head in the doorway. "Uh, Quinn? Uncle Umbridge is here with some guy I don't recognize."

"Fuck," Quinn says, pushing to his feet.

"Who's Uncle Umbridge?" I whisper to Harrison.

"Our dad's brother. He's an ass. Thus, the nickname. His name is actually Uncle Lewis, but we call him Umbridge, and our grandfather is Voldemort."

I snort because that's pretty hilarious. "I have an evil uncle too, and I never once thought to call him anything so clever."

"Harrison!" Quinn calls. "You and Birdie are going to want to come here."

My heart pounds, and I look at Harrison to see if he knows what's going on but he seems as confused as me. He threads our fingers together as we leave the kitchen area. The minute we breach the living room, it feels like something is squeezing my chest.

I eye the two men standing near the front

door. One is unfamiliar, and I assume he's the uncle Harrison spoke of. The other man is tall and impeccably dressed, I know him. He sees me, and his eyes flick briefly to my hand in Harrison's.

"Princess Beatrice, it seems I have finally found you. Thanks to the very helpful online gossip rag called the *Saddle Peek*, is it?"

"Damn, that was my fault," Madison admits.

I wince.

"Did he just call you princess?" Harrison asks.

"Oh shit," Hayes whispers from behind us and I know the rest of the Crawford siblings have followed us into the room.

"Mr. Whittenborg, that is not my title, and you know it."

The older man raises one thin brow. "As the official betrothed of the crown prince of Saldania, you are his princess."

"She's my wife," Harrison says, taking a step forward.

"I beg your pardon," the man says, barely sparing Harrison a glance. "She cannot be your wife when she is engaged to someone else."

"In this country, the only thing that matters is the wedding ceremony. She said her vows with me nearly nine months ago." Harrison's eyes narrow on the other man. "You have no authority over her here."

I squeeze Harrison's hand. "Maybe we should go talk privately for a few minutes."

He nods. "We can. Won't change anything, though." He glances at Quinn. "You got this for a bit?"

Quinn nods.

Harrison and I climb the stairs to our bedroom, and it's a far cry from the exuberance we felt the night before. Once we're inside the room, I motion for him to sit on the bed.

"There's a lot you never told me," he says.

I wince. "Just the precise details. I told you my family had arranged for me to marry an important man."

"A prince."

"Yes. A prince. It's a very small country and the monarchy isn't that different from England's. It's mostly a figurehead with very little political power." I shake my head. "Regardless of any of that, I didn't want it. I wanted to move to America and go to university and write my games. I'm sorry I didn't tell you everything."

"I can't compete with a fucking prince, Birdie." He rubs a hand over his face.

My heart stops. "This is all so much drama and fuss I've brought into your life. I'm so sorry, Harrison. I can leave. We can get an annulment and I'll disappear from your life."

He stands and then he's backing me up against the door. "What the fuck are you talking about?"

"I know you don't like drama and, oh my goodness, this is the very definition of drama. This isn't what you signed up for." I know I've got tears in my eyes, and I can't do anything about it. It breaks my heart to leave because I've fallen in love with my husband.

"Birdie, I don't care if a new prince shows up on this doorstep every day for the rest of our lives claiming to be engaged to you. I don't care if I have to learn to fence so I can beat them all in duels or whatever the hell they do with those tiny swords. You are *my* wife and I'm not letting you go." He leans down a little and cups my face so we meet eye to eye. "Drama or no drama. I'm all in, baby."

I release a watery laugh. "Are you sure? Because that right there was as strong as I'm going get in offering to leave you."

"You don't want to leave me?"

"Never. I love you, Harrison. I know it's soon and you probably think I'm crazy, but I don't care. I'm in love with you. And I want this marriage to be for real and for forever. Not because I'm escaping my country or you're trying to save your family's ranch. I want us to pick each other because we belong together. I know we can't do that because our situations are what they are, but I wish that's how it was."

He gives me a quick kiss. "I don't ever want to be

apart from you again, Birdie. So I hope Mike is okay with you doing satellite work from the ranch."

"Mike will be fine. I own the controlling shares of the company."

"For the record. It's not too soon. I love you too, wife. Our marriage is absolutely the real kind and it's gonna last forever."

eighteen
...

HARRISON

Initially, I wanted today to be a complete surprise for Birdie. But my sister made it very clear that you cannot surprise a woman with a wedding. There are decisions only the bride can make. And since this is to be a make-up wedding of sorts for us, Birdie deserved to make those choices.

Like the dress. And the cake. And the venue.

All valid points. Sometimes, having a sister is a good thing.

I thought for sure Birdie would want to get married at one of the big churches, but she picked the courtyard of Gator's the Cajun restaurant in town. I grew up with the Guidry kids, so it was easy enough to call their parents and make the reservations.

Birdie's parents flew in for the ceremony. I'm not sure if they're happy that she's staying married to a Texas rancher, but she didn't give them much of a choice.

I'm wearing what's known in Texas as a cowboy's tuxedo—starched and pressed Wranglers, clean boots, a tuxedo shirt, bowtie, and a black jacket with tails. And my black Stetson is sitting securely on my head.

Hayes sticks his head in the makeshift groom's room. "You ready?"

"Yeah. I'm ready."

"Let's get you married, then."

"Maybe you'll be next."

He puts a hand over his heart. "It would make all the single women cry if I was taken."

I shake my head, grabbing my guitar as I leave the room. "Did you make sure there was a stool out there for me?"

"Yes. That's taken care of, and I have the ring safely in my pocket." He pats his chest.

We might have our differences, but there wasn't another choice for my best man.

He nods at my guitar. "Does she know?"

"I don't think so. I've had a hell of a time practicing since we're together most of the time. I'm sure the guys and the cattle are tired of hearing me sing."

Hayes chuckles. "No one deserves happiness the way you do, brother. I hope you know that." He pats me on the shoulder, and we make our way to the front of aisle.

Madison comes down first, and then there she is. My Birdie, a vision in pink. Because, of course, she's wearing a pink wedding gown. God, I love that woman. It looks like a traditional wedding dress in shape and style, but it's the color of bubble gum.

She smiles broadly at me.

I love you, I mouth to her.

I love you, she mouths back.

Yeah, we're that couple. Get over it. Life is awesome.

When she reaches me I kiss her hand. "You look gorgeous, baby."

"Thank you."

I turn to face our guests. "Birdie and I want to thank everyone for coming to our second wedding. It's nice to get to share this one with our friends and family. Before I pass the mic over to the preacher, I have something I want to share with my wife. If y'all will indulge me."

Birdie looks at me curiously until I reach behind me and grab my guitar. Instantly, her eyes fill with tears.

"I'm not much of a songwriter, but I've done my best to put into words what you mean to me."

I start the song. The guitar intro isn't very long, and I keep my eyes locked on my beautiful bride as I sing her what's in my heart.

> If I had a choice
> I'd stay forever in your arms
> If heaven is a place
> I'd go with your name on my lips
> If I could sing my way into eternity
> I would, with you by my side
> You're my hope
> My inspiration
> My soul
> My peace
> If I had a choice
> I'd stay forever in this memory
> with you, baby,
> with you

Once I'm done, I hand Hayes my guitar and go stand next to Birdie. The preacher moves in front of us and then we're reciting our vows, promising to love each other until death parts us. I think I might hold on even after that because there will never be another woman for me.

"You may kiss your bride."

I don't waste another moment before I cup her face and lower my lips to hers. Every kiss feels as magical as the first. That spark, that sizzle that ignites every time we touch.

Cheers go up and my brothers start cat-calling and heckling for us to "get a room."

So we do, and we make love all night long.

epilogue

. . .

Lone Star Husband

BIRDIE

It's been a few weeks since our second wedding and although we haven't had a chance to take a honeymoon, I feel very much like a newlywed. Even with Harrison working longer shifts on the ranch, we still make time every day to connect and talk. We still have so much to learn about one another, but the longing only grows stronger the more time we spend together.

I come out of the bathroom after a nice long bubble soak to find Harrison sitting on the edge of the bed, towel wrapped around his waist, hair damp.

"You could have come in and joined me," I say.

He gives me a wicked grin that immediately has all my lady bits coming to attention. "I had other plans. So I took a quick shower downstairs."

"You look tired, my love." I go to him and rub his shoulders while he faceplants into my cleavage.

"Two more calves today. I don't know why our births are late this year. Guess the bulls decided to get busy a little later than usual. Normally, we have a straggler or two, but we're done calving by the beginning of March."

"Would you like me to give you a massage?"

"There's actually something I've been thinking about all day. Something you told me a while ago." He scoots himself back so he's lying on our bed, his head almost to the wall. "Come here." He pats his chest.

I crawl up to lie on his pectorals. It's one of my favorite places to be.

"No, baby. Come sit on your throne. I want to eat that pretty pussy and I want you riding my face while I do it."

I suck in a breath. I told him that particular fantasy the first night we made love. "You've eaten me out before."

"Yes, but in different positions. Right now, I want your pussy right here." He touches his lips.

"You sure I won't be too heavy? I don't want to suffocate you."

"First of all, that would be the best fucking way to die. Ever. Case closed. Secondly, do I look like I don't know how to breathe through my nose, Birdie?" He gives me a lopsided grin, one that makes him look boyish and charming. "I'll figure it out before I die from lack of oxygen. Promise."

I let go of my towel and move further up the bed so I can straddle his face. He wraps his arms around my thighs and pulls me down directly on his mouth. The first brush of his wicked tongue and my head lolls back.

I moan. It doesn't take long for us to find a rhythm, or rather, for me to shamelessly grind my pussy on his face while I brace my hands on the wall.

"Harrison, your tongue feels so good," I gasp.

He reaches one hand up and squeezes my breast, flicking and pinching my nipples into hard tips. Still, I ride his face. He groans underneath me and the vibration shudders through my clit.

I lean up on my knees and then turn my body around so I'm facing his cock. It's barely covered by the towel. I wrap my hand around his thick shaft and pump him once, twice.

Harrison moans into my pussy.

Leaning forward, I suck the tip into my mouth. He's so damn big, I can't get much of him in my mouth, but I can suck that tip like it's my job.

He smacks my ass and increases his licking, flicking his tongue at double the speed he was going.

I'm getting so close and it's hard to concentrate on what I'm doing, but I do my best. Swirling my tongue over the head of his cock, flicking my tongue into the hole, and swallowing the pre-cum that's leaking there.

I cup his balls with my other hand, fondling them as he rocks his pelvis upward, effectively fucking my mouth. I let my jaw go loose and concentrate on what he's doing to my pussy so I won't choke and gag on his length.

Harrison sucks my clit into his mouth. He pulls and pulls on that bundle of nerves until my orgasm crashes through me. I shriek and release his cock in time for him to come all over my boobs, the warm ropes of his cum painting my skin.

I collapse onto the bed next to him. "I love you, Harrison Crawford."

"I love you, Birdie Crawford." He leans up on his elbows. "In fact, you're the love of my life. Also, I could eat that fucking pussy every day."

"I think that might kill me."

"Haven't we already established that it would be the very best way to go?"

acknowledgments

Special thanks for the ridiculously talented and generous Nichole Rose for letting me borrow her poem to use as part of Harrison's song to Birdie.

lone star boss

. . .

Quinn

The minute I see Amber fending off handsy customers at the small-town diner, I know she needs protection. So I do the only logical thing, I bring her home to be my live-in housekeeper and cook. She's too young and innocent for me, but every day is a battle not to claim her. I know this much, if I can't keep my hands to myself, I either have to marry her or send her far away.

Amber

I'm used to being on my own. I've been alone in the world since I was fourteen. I like my independence, and I don't need anyone tell me what to do. I don't care how hot they look in a pair of cowboy boots. Except when it comes to Quinn Crawford. There is something in that bossy tone of his that makes my body—and my heart—crave him.

nineteen

. . .

Quinn

I can't take my eyes off of her.

My buddy Blake and I met for drinks and food at a joint outside of Saddle Creek. I wanted to be able to discuss my family's current situation without tidbits of the conversation showing up on the local gossip board, *the Saddle Peek*.

My siblings and I just found out that our grandfather—who could die at any moment—stipulated in his will that if we aren't married at the time of his death, we'll lose our family ranch.

The ranch I've devoted my entire life to. Where I live and work and someday aim to raise kids with the woman I love.

Of course, all my plans and goals in life got thrown out the window when I heard about my grandfather's will. Since I'm still trying to wrap my brain around the news, the last thing I need is some sweet thing distracting me. And yet, here I am, sitting across from my best friend Blake, at some rundown hole in the wall called *Earl's Eats* about forty miles outside of town, trying to concentrate on him explaining some legal crap to me. And all I can do is stare at her. The waitress to be exact. The gorgeous waitress across the room.

She's a tiny little thing. Obviously young too. But the nonstop curves on her compact body make it known that she is very much an adult.

"Then I could get nekkid and dance around like a chicken. You think that would work?" Blake asks.

I turn to face him. "What the fuck are you even talking about?"

He tosses his arms up. "Exactly. You asked me to meet you here so we could talk without eavesdroppers and yet you're not listening to me at all. Because all you can do is watch that sweet piece of ass move around the room."

"Don't call her that," I snap. But my voice comes out more like a growl.

Blake's brows nearly crawl into his hairline. I instantly regret opening my damn mouth. In all our years of friendship, I have never once reacted like that over a woman.

Before I can shrug off my reaction—or better yet, apologize—she's standing at our table.

"What can I get you boys?" she asks. Her short frame means her tits are pretty much at my eye level while she's standing next to us. Short, but stacked with curves in all the right places. A little plump and soft in the best possible way. Her golden hair falls down her back in soft waves. And that heart-shaped face of hers—well I'm pretty sure hundreds of years ago men would have written poems about her beauty. Me? I just sit here and stare like I'm an idiot.

She might as well have wings and a halo, her voice is so sweet and pure.

I just stare at her.

I know she's asked a question, but I've evidently lost my mind and can't remember how to talk.

Blake, smirking like a smug son of a bitch, says, "We'll take a couple of Shiners." He winks. "And we'll need a minute to figure out what to order."

Before she walks away though, she looks at me with her pretty waitress smile. But as soon as our eyes meet, that smile falters. Her throat bobs as she swallows hard.

I know she feels whatever I've been feeling since I first laid eyes on her. A zing of recognition that hits me straight in the gut.

But fast on the heels of that is another realization. Now that she's standing this close to me, I know for sure. She's way too damn young for me.

"I'll be right back with your beers," she says, her gaze lingering on mine for just a moment before she walks away, her steps slower at first, like she's struggling to break free of the gravitational pull of that moment when our eyes met.

"Dude, that was like watching, I don't know, grandma porn."

"What the fuck does that mean?" I ask.

"You know, it's like all intense and hot and shit. But nobody's naked."

I'm already shaking my head before he even finishes his dumbass sentence. "Okay, that's not a thing and I don't want to ever hear those words come out of your mouth again. Besides, that's not what is happening. She's just … she's very pretty, but she's also very young," I say as much to remind myself as to declare it to Blake.

Blake is still grinning. "She's not too young if she can work in a bar."

"People work around that shit all the time. You know that."

"True. But I'm not gonna get up and go ask to see all their licenses to make sure everything is in order. But I can tell she's an adult, even if that means she's a young one."

"If she's not old enough to rent a car, then she's too young for me," I say.

"That is the most asinine thing you've ever said."

I'm about to argue when she returns with our beers. "Do you know what else you boys want?"

Yeah, I want to take you home and fuck you six ways

to Sunday. That's what I want, angel baby. I want you naked and spread all over my house.

But I don't say that. I just stare at her again, because I evidently don't know how to talk anymore.

Blake chuckles. "We'll just take two fully loaded cheeseburgers."

She gives me a look, like she's waiting for me to say something. When I don't, she spins around and leaves the table again.

"Dude, you can't even talk. I mean, I've never seen you like this. All through high school, you were all top man on campus. You could talk to any chick."

"That's not just any chick." I jab my finger into the tabletop.

"Well, then talk to her; bring her home."

Yeah, there are a thousand reasons why that's a shitty idea. Starting with she's too young for me and ending with this bullshit with my grandfather's will. I need to get serious about finding a wife or my future will be screwed. I do not have time for this.

But that doesn't keep me from watching as she approaches another table. It's a round table of guys about our age, maybe a little older. And they're handsy. She's smiling it off, smacking their hands away, dancing around the table so that she can get away from the one that clearly has some sort of problem with hearing the word no.

I'm seconds from getting to my feet, but then she leaves the table and is off to the kitchen.

"That shit is not okay," I say.

"No, it's not," Blake agrees.

"That happens again, and I'm putting a stop to it."

It does happen again. And I don't put a stop to it. Not because I don't want to. But because she's deft at putting a stop to it on her own, and she's quick about it, rendering me useless. Which frankly pisses me off. If this shit happens every night that she works—it turns my stomach to even think of her having to fend off this many advances every damn night.

So when she approaches our table to bring our burgers, I've had enough.

I look up and catch her eye. "What's your name, angel?"

"Amber." She puts her hand on her hip, not moving even an inch away from me. "What's yours, cowboy?"

"Quincy, but everyone calls me Quinn."

Just then, Blake's phone rings. He grabs it off the table and is answering it before he even walks away.

"What can I do for you, Quinn?" she asks, propping her hip against the edge of the table like she's settling in to chat.

"I just thought I'd warn you that I'm about to cause some trouble on your behalf."

Her brows raise and she gives me a grin. "Are you, now?"

"Because I don't like men putting their hands on

you. And clearly they don't know how to hear the word no."

An expression flickers across her face that I can't quite read. Like she's surprised and a little amused. She pats my shoulder. "That's very sweet of you to try to come to my rescue, but I promise, I can take care of myself."

"You put up with this kind of thing every night?"

She shrugs, which is as a good as admitting that yes, she does. "Just part of the job."

"Sounds like you need a better job."

She laughs, a sound that's unexpectedly husky given how sweet her speaking voice is. "I'd take one if I could get it. But good jobs around here are hard to find."

Just then, Blake returns to the table. Right in time for him to hear the end of our conversation.

"You should give her a job, Quinn," he says, sliding into the booth.

"What?" I snap.

Amber raises her eyebrows in surprise, looking from me to Blake and back again.

"You should give her a job," he repeats slowly. He takes a long draw on his beer, not bothering to hide his smug grin. "You've been saying for months now that you need to hire a housekeeper."

"No, I haven't."

"Yeah. You have." He looks at Amber and starts chatting with her like he's conducting a damn job interview. "Quinn and his siblings own and run The Little C Ranch down near Saddle Peak. Quinn, Harrison, and Roe all live on the ranch and they need a cook and housekeeper."

"No, we don't. Roe got married and moved in with his wife."

But the rest is true. And our youngest brother is coming home from college soon. Also, I have been saying it for months. But now? Faced with the prospect of Amber filling that position. Je-sus. This is the last damn thing I need.

Blake ignores me. "What do you think, Amber? That sound like something you could do?"

She gives him a long look, before turning those clear blue eyes in my direction. There's a question there in her gaze, like she's waiting for me to comment. After a beat, she flashes Blake a superficial smile. "I think I don't want to be the object of anyone's charity. Besides, I'm a damn good cook so I doubt he could afford me."

"Oh, if anyone needs charity, it's Quinn," Blake says smoothly. "You should see what his cooking is like. It's a miracle he hasn't starved to death, yet. Besides, if we have to sit here and watch those guys harass you all night, he might have an aneurysm."

"I'm not going to have a damn aneurysm," I grumble.

I can't make any promises about my behavior

though, because I just might lose my shit if those guys keep putting their hands on her.

As if Blake can read my mind, he says, "Yeah, he'd probably do something stupid to defend your honor though, and then I'd have to clean up his mess." Shaking his head, he adds, "I'll have to bail him out of jail. And I really don't want to have to do that."

"You boys are a riot. I've got to get back to work though because Earl is over there giving me the stink eye." She tilts her head in the direction of the bar.

Sure enough there's a crusty old guy behind the bar, arms folded over his beer belly, and a scowl aimed straight at Amber.

As calm and confident as she was dealing with the customers, something in her gaze goes skittish when she glances at her boss. That something raises all kinds of alarm bells in my head.

"Does he put his hands on you, too?" I ask.

She shivers at my question, but tries to hide it behind a smile and chuckle as she shakes her head.

"Amber, now!" Earl shouts from across the small restaurant, and I see her flinch.

"Amber, honey," Blake says, "could you get our burgers packed up to go?"

She frowns. "Uh, sure."

But I'm already across the room with my fist tangled in Earl's greasy shirt. I yank him halfway onto the bar.

"You giving her shit about talking to us when we were trying to do your job!" I demand.

"I don't know what you're talking about," Earl mutters.

"You don't see all the men in this establishment of yours putting their hands all over your waitress here? Your underage waitress, I'm guessing."

"Who? Amber?" he gasps. "She's nineteen. She's of age!"

"Sure, to wait tables, not to serve alcohol. How about I put a call in to the liquor licensing bureau and have them check on the employment records. I'm thinking she's not old enough to have served me that piss water you call beer."

"Now hold up a minute!" This comes from Amber who is now by my side. "Put him down."

I glance down at her. I don't loosen my grip on the man's shirt until I see she's okay.

I release him with a shove and the man falls to the floor in a heap of body odor and grunts. "You're fired. You've been a pain in my ass since the moment I hired you. Shoulda fired you after you broke Larry's finger last week."

"He deserved that!" Amber yells. Then she turns on me, her scowl making the skin above her chest and her cheeks pink. "Well, I guess you've just got yourself a new employee. Just what will I be doing for you?"

"Cooking and cleaning, like Blake said. If you

don't know how to do any of that, you can learn there."

She takes off her waitress apron and tosses it over the bar. Then she grabs one of the tall glasses filled with bills and change where people have stuffed tips. "I'll consider this my severance package."

"In that case, grab both of them." I nod to the other glass.

She does and then we're out the door right before I'm certain a riot is about to start.

twenty

. . .

Amber

One month later…

A month into my job as housekeeper and cook for the Little C Ranch, I'm starting to wonder if I'm as stupid as Earl always said I was.

Okay, not really, because I know Earl was a jerk and a moron and that him calling me stupid was just his way of excusing the fact that he skimmed money out of the tip jar.

Still, what exactly am I doing here?

It's been a month since Quinn "rescued" me from Earl's. That first night, he drove me home to the little apartment I used to rent in Cactus Ridge. The place was a dump, but I could walk to the grocery store and to work and it was cheap, so it had that going for it.

On the drive, Quinn had assured me that he'd come back the next day to help me pack up my belongings and then get me settled at his ranch. Then he took one look at the apartment and refused to leave me there alone overnight. So I'd packed up my duffle bag of clothes, and my two milk crates of belongings, and we'd been in Saddle Creek by midnight.

I know it sounds crazy meeting a guy in a bar, accepting a job from him, and moving into his house five hours later.

But my granny always said, when you know, you know.

She believed that Tabasco makes everything better, the only flour for biscuits is White Lily, and that true love hits you hard and fast.

I've known for years Granny was dead to rights about Tabasco and White Lily flour, so when I met Quinn and instantly felt like I'd been hit on the head with an Acme love anvil, I figured she was right about that too.

So when he offered me a job and place to live, I grabbed it, because life is too short not to trust your gut.

That's another thing Granny used to say.

But now I'm second-guessing everything.

I moved into Quinn's house, assuming he felt

that same Acme Anvil of love that I'd felt. I figured offering me a job was just an excuse to keep me close. I figured he'd eventually make a move on me. I mean, I'd seen the hungry way his eyes raked over my body that night in Earl's. How he'd stared, wordlessly, until other men had touched me and then Quinn had been full of protective, bossy words.

Words that had woken up my body in a way I'd never experienced. How my skin had felt warm, my breath had sped up, and my breasts felt heavy. I've been aroused before, but this was that plus. Like I'd gone to the local fast food place and they asked me if I wanted to supersize my order. If it looks like Quinn Crawford, yes, please. Extra sauce on the side.

In the time I've worked here, I've made approximately a hundred meals. I've cleaned the entire house top to bottom. I've planted an herb garden. I've perfected my granny's biscuit recipe. I've taught myself how to make homemade bread—which is what I'm currently doing. I've spent countless hours trying to befriend the barn cat who wants nothing to do with me. I've learned how to take care of chickens. I've started a compost pile.

And—I'm not making this up—not one, but two of Quinn's brothers have fallen in love and gotten married. Or gotten married and then fallen in love. Okay technically Roe was already married when I got here, but still it was like a couple weeks before.

Either way, it's like a veritable Las Vegas wedding chapel around here.

You know what has not happened in the month I've lived here?

Quinn has not made a move on me.

Not a single move.

He hasn't so much as inched in my direction.

Oh, sure. I still feel all the zings.

And I'd swear on my granny's cast iron skillet that Quinn feels them too.

So why hasn't he kissed me yet?

I give the dough I'm kneading a punch—since I can't very well punch anything else—and mutter, "What is wrong with me?"

"Nothing's wrong with you," says a feminine voice from behind me.

I whirl around to see Birdie standing in the kitchen doorway.

She's still dressed in her jammies and obviously just woke up.

Birdie is Harrison's wife. They gotten married a few years ago so she could get a green card or something, but they didn't live together until recently when this mess with the Crawfords' grandfather's messed up will came out.

She's beautiful and practically royalty from some European country I'd never heard of before now. And she designs computer games for a living. So, basically, she's the coolest person I've ever met. With this fancy, posh accent and she says funny things like 'bugger' and 'rubbish' and 'knickers.'

She also works long and odd hours—which apparently is something all programmers do—which explains why she's only now coming downstairs for breakfast, even though it's nearly noon.

Now, she's staring at me like she thinks I'm crazy. Not that I blame her, since she just walked in on me talking to a bowl of bread dough.

"What?" I ask, hoping she'll just let it go.

"You asked what was wrong with you," she explains in her delightful accent. "And I said nothing is wrong with you."

"Hmm …" I murmur, now hoping that she'll let this go.

No such luck.

She slides onto the stool by the kitchen counter and props her chin in her hands, blinking sleepily. "Why would think something is wrong with you?"

Automatically, I wipe the dough off my hands and turn on the tea kettle to make her tea.

"You don't have to do that," she says quickly. "You don't have to make me tea."

I wave aside her comment. "It's literally my job. I'm the cook."

Worried my tone sounds bitter, I smile at her. Smiling at Birdie is easy, since she's ridiculously nice. Not feeling bitter about my job is a tad harder.

I don't mind hard work. I've worked hard my

whole life. And my job here at the Little C is by far the easiest job I've ever had. I get decent pay. I don't have to cover my own rent. I've even been saving to take some online classes so I can get my degree.

It's not the job I'm bitter about. It's the lack of Quinn I'm bitter about.

Even though I don't say any of this out loud, Birdie nods like she can read my mind. "This is about Quinn, isn't it?"

"How'd you guess?" The kettle starts whining, so I pour the hot water into a cup and then slide it in front of her.

Instead of answering my question, she drops a tea bag in and asks, "How long have you worked here now?"

"Thirty-two days."

"Hmm …" she gives her tea a stir with her spoon. "And how long have you been in love with Quinn?"

I gasp feeling like I've been punched. She quirks an eyebrow, clearly prepared to wait for my answer.

Finally, I admit, "Thirty-two and half days."

"That's what I thought." She wraps her hands around her mug and brings it up to her lips to blow on. "What exactly are you going to do about that?"

I throw up my hands in frustration. "That's the point! I don't know what to do about it! I thought there was chemistry between us. I was so sure of it. That's why I moved in here when he offered me the job. But, it turns out, he really just wanted a housekeeper and a cook."

She's shaking her head. "Negative, Ghost Rider. Quinn's just being stubborn. I've seen the way he looks at you."

I eye her suspiciously. What I want to do is yell, "Tell me more! How does he look at me? How do you know? I need details!"

I'm still trying to figure out how to say this without sounding needy, when Birdie sends me a sly look.

"Moreover, I've seen the way *you* look at him."

I give her the side eye. "What do you mean?"

She leans forward and props her elbows on the counter, cupping her mug in her hands. "Okay, is it time for straight talk? Are we there yet?"

I blow out a breath. Are we there yet?

This is a tough one for me. Birdie is lovely, but I've know her less than a month.

Okay, yeah. I just admitted to feeling like I know Quinn is the one after only a few minutes, but this is different. I don't have a lot of experience with female friendships. For so long, it was just me and Granny. I don't know that I've a friend I could confide in since … well, since Granny.

Even though I think Birdie is about the coolest woman I've ever met, I hesitate a moment before nodding. "Okay, Yeah. We're there. Hit me with the straight talk."

"You want Quinn, right?"

"Yes." This time, there's no hesitation. Because I know what I want. I want him. I'm all in.

"Okay, then you and I need to talk."

"We've been talking since you came down for breakfast."

"No, we've been chatting since I came down. Now, we need to talk. About something important."

"Oooookay…" I draw out my response.

"Harrison and I are going out of town." She waves her hand dismissively. "Because I have this Comic Con thing I have to go to in San Diego."

Again … Really? "This Comic Con thing" … as if going to Comic Con as a game designer isn't cool.

She blows right past that detail.

"We're gonna just make a honeymoon out of it. And we're gonna be out of this house for a week. Which means…" Birdie stops talking and makes a motion with her hand like I'm supposed to fill in the blank.

"Which means?" I ask.

"It means that you and Quinn will be alone in the house. And y'all can finally stop dancing around all this attraction and you can make a move."

She shakes her head. "Because I have to tell you, he's never going to make a move. He's never going to take the first step. Because he has had some stick up his ass about how old you are and how old he is and how that's somehow inappropriate."

"The age thing?" I ask. "*That's* what's holding him up? I'm perfectly legal. I'm nearly twenty. And I've been on my own for years."

"I know that he knows that. But still. He has a hang up about the age difference. So if you want him—and I know you do—and he wants you because I've seen it—then you're gonna have to be the one to make the move. You have to push his buttons and break him."

"How do I do that?"

"Good grief. Don't you watch porn? Just do that."

"No! I don't watch porn. My granny would have swatted my behind if she'd even heard you talking about that!"

"Well, your granny's not here."

"No. She passed a couple of years ago."

"Okay, well, now I feel like a jerk. My point is, you need to get some gumption and make a damn move."

"I literally don't know how to do that."

Shaking her head, she sighs. "Okay, I'm sending you a list of books."

"Books?" I ask skeptically. She already has her phone out and she's tapping away on it. "Like instructional guides?" If we're doing straight talk, I might as well be honest here. "Because I don't have a lot of experience with men."

Her lips quirk. "Yeah. I figured as much when you admitted you hadn't ever watched porn. And no, not an instructional guide. I'm going to send you a list of romance novels to read."

"How is that going to help?"

"Trust me." She rubs her hands together and then hits send with a dramatic flourish. An instant later, the phone Quinn bought me on my second day here dings in my pocket. Birdie beams at me. "Go read. And then make your move."

twenty-one

...

Quinn

My brother, Harrison, and I are busy mending fences around the fence on the back pasture.

Harrison throws down the pliers in a huff. "Are you gonna tell me about the bug that crawled up your ass and died?"

I just stare at him. "What is that even supposed to mean?"

"For starters,"—he props his elbow on the nearest fence post and nudges back his hat with the back of his other hand—"You've been attacking this fence repair like it's the one thing you were put on this planet to do."

I scowl at him. "You and Birdie are leaving in the

morning. If we're going to get this done before you leave, then now's the time."

"Well, sure. But this has been on the to-do list for a six months."

I ignore him, pull my own pliers out of my back pocket and get to work doing the job he stopped doing to chat.

"My point is, this job could have waited. But you're blowing through work like you're worried demons will cart you off if you stand still too long. And you're in an even worse mood than usual. Didn't you go out last night?"

"Yes, I did."

"Get laid?"

"Not your business."

"That means no."

Of course it means no. I haven't touched a woman in ages. Years. But I'm sure not going to tell one of my younger brothers that. Especially not one recently in love and having all the sex. Meanwhile, it's a miracle my poor dick hasn't rusted and fallen off.

I bracket my arms on the fence post. "Last night Eileen Perry ended up at my table and she was laying down some pretty thick hints."

Eileen Perry was a few years before me in high school. Head cheerleader, hot as hell. Every teenage guy's wet dream. Now, she's divorced and everyone in town knows she's looking for husband number two. Or, hell, maybe it's number three. I haven't been keeping track. Ever since the news broke in the *Saddle Peek* about all of us Crawfords needing to get hitched, she's been around every time I turn the corner.

"You just weren't picking them up." He visibly shudders. "Don't blame you. I wouldn't be surprised if her vagina had teeth."

"Christ, Harrison, I do not need that image in my mind. She's not that bad."

"If you say so."

"Well, I need a wife." I ignore the way my heart whispers a certain name as if chanting it again and again will make me act on something I know is wrong.

It's his turn to stare at me.

"What?"

"I know you see it. Everyone sees it. Just marry Amber," he says.

He just tosses that out as if he didn't just suggest I marry a goddamn teenager. "She's nineteen. I'm thirty-one." I shake my head. "Just because I'm attracted to her doesn't mean I should be."

"It's not illegal."

"Well, maybe it should be."

Harrison pulls a glove off and scratches at the back of his neck. "So your solution is to possibly hook up with Eileen Perry? Do you like her? Are you even attracted to her?"

My stomach knots. "It doesn't matter. The point is that according to our selfish grandfather's trust, we all have to be married. And we need to do it before he dies, which could be any day. Eileen makes more sense. She's closer to my age. She's an adult."

"She has a teenage son I've heard is a menace. Roe said that Callie's brother is dealing with him and his buddies at least once a week in the Sheriff's office." Harrison explains, mentioning one of our other brother's wife whose, whose brother is the local sheriff.

I don't want to parent a rowdy teenager. "I could handle him. I managed to get you and Hayes and Johnny into adulthood."

"Fuck you, brother. I was the easy one. And I'm barely six years younger than you." Harrison leans forward, bracing one of his booted feet on the bottom rung of the fence. "Let me ask you this. Do you like Amber? Are you attracted to her?"

"Yes. She's all I can think of."

"What do you think when you look at her?"

"Mine. She's fucking mine." I take off my hat and wipe my brow. "But none of that matters. Because she doesn't belong to me. She deserves better. Someone close to her age." Someone who doesn't want to dirty her up and do filthy things to her. She's an angel and I'm a devil for the filth I want to do to her sweet curves.

I don't say any of this out loud, obviously, but this conversation is done. "Let it go. We've got too much work to do before you leave to stand around gossiping like a bunch of old ladies at church."

Harrison must see the resolve in my gaze, but he just shakes his head. "Jesus," he mutters, bending down to pick up the pliers. "And I always thought Hayes was the dumb one in the family."

twenty-two

Lone Star BOSS

Amber

I stand in my room looking at myself in the mirror. I snap a picture and immediately send it to Birdie.

> *Me: <pic of me>*
> *Me: Do I look as stupid as I feel?*
> *Birdie: NO! Damn, girl, you look hot. Want me to ask Harrison's opinion?*
> *Me: Please don't. This is embarrassing enough as it is.*
> *Birdie: You've got this. You look like a sex kitten.*
> *Me: Or Daisy Duke's drug addicted little sister.*

Birdie: LOL. Not true. But that was funny.
Birdie: Do you want him?
Me: More than anything.
Birdie: Do you believe you belong together?
Me: Yes, I really do.
Birdie: Then go seduce that man!
Me: Thank you. Sorry to bug you on your honeymoon.
Birdie: It's really a work trip, we're just pretending it's a honeymoon.

I look at my reflection again. My ass is practically hanging out of the bottom of my denim shorts. And my size C plus boobs strain against the white of my tank top. I don't normally free-boob it; I'm a bra-wearing kinda of gal. But desperate times call for desperate measures.

I've got a week to make Quinn see that we belong together.

I run back down the stairs to make the finishing touches on dinner. They're supposed to be quitting early today because one of the new ranch hands is getting married out of town.

I've made all his favorites for dinner. About a week after I got here, I found his mama's old recipe book and I've been slowly making my way through it. She cooked a lot like my Granny, and I don't know,

I kinda feel like I've gotten to know her in a way by flipping through that old book. All her handwritten notes in the margins. Sticky notes stuck to pages to remind her which kid wanted which cake for their birthday.

Though in Quinn's case, he prefers pie. Pecan pie to be exact. Made with pecans harvested off this very property, too. I wasn't here back in late fall, early winter when they would have been picked and put up. But I have sure made use of the stash I found in the deep freeze. Last week, I chopped some up and put them in some homemade sticky buns.

I know the night that Quinn brought me here, the night he "saved" me, he didn't care if I knew a kitchen from a garage. There was no way for him to know I've been on my own since I was sixteen. That I'd been cooking with my Granny since I could reach the countertops in her old two bedroom home. Even I didn't know at the time how much I would love puttering around the kitchen, getting up early enough to make breakfast for Quinn and Harrison before they head out to work. Making a big mess of food for them and the ranch hands at lunch.

I've taken to this life like it's what I was born to do. I've fallen in love with this old house and the lovely family memories that seem steeped in the walls. It feels like home in a way nothing has since Granny died.

And, yes, I know some of that is because it is a *real* home. The first real home I've had since Granny died. But most of it is because this is Quinn's home and my heart already feels like home is wherever he is.

Gravel crunches beneath tires outside and I know that means Quinn is home. Butterflies launch into flight in my belly, but I keep myself busy in the kitchen, finishing up everything. He'll want to shower before he eats. Not that I care one way or another. I'm so desperate for him to touch me, he could come in covered in mud and I'd still want to be pressed up against his huge, muscular frame.

He's not built like a body-builder or a gym rat. No, Quinn's body is sculpted from lifting hay bales and feed bags and hauling baby calves when necessary.

Normally he'll come in, bark a greeting in the general direction of kitchen, then head to his room for a shower. But today he says nothing and I just hear his feet stomp down the hall, then his bedroom door slams.

So he's not in a great mood. I've dealt with Quinn moody before. Hell, Quinn is always moody. Growly, grumpy, scowl-y, he's like the Seven Dwarfs of a bad mood.

Fifteen minutes later I'm pouring him a fresh glass of iced tea when he barges into the eat-in kitchen area. He stops cold at the sight of me. My back is to him, but I hear the shock in the sudden halt of his footsteps. I turn to face him, holding out the glass of iced tea. His eyes land on my face.

"Goddammit," he mutters, then shoves himself down into his chair. "What the fuck are you wearing?"

I ignore him and set down his plate and glass of tea. "I made all your favorites tonight, cowboy."

He tears his eyes off of me long enough to glance at his plate. He grunts in response, and just starts eating.

Which is fine. I know when he comes home from working the cattle he's ravenous. And his body will need fuel for what I have planned. Do I actually know what I'm doing? Nope, no clue. But I've read enough of Birdie's books she sent me to get the gist of how seductions go. Though admittedly, the man is usually the one doing the seducing. Just goes to show that I'm dumb enough to fall for the most stubborn man in the world.

I finish my plate, I didn't eat very much because I don't want to have gas or something the first time I have sex. That would be so embarrassing.

"This was good, angel, damn good," he murmurs.

My nipples pebble at the sound of that nickname. He hasn't called me 'angel' again since that first night. He's nearly slipped up a few times, but he always ends up using my name.

I bring over the slice of pie. "I hope you saved room for pie." I set it down in front of him after removing his empty dinner plate.

He looks down, then back up at me. "Did you make my mama's pecan pie?" His voice sounds thick with emotion.

"I sure did. I can't promise it'll be as good as hers, but here, let's taste." I fork up a bite from his slice and bring the utensil to his full lips.

He obediently opens and then he moans as he chews. His eyes close. "Amber, what are you doing?"

I push the table back enough so that I can squeeze in between him and the heavy oak. Then I straddle his lap. His hands immediately grip my hips and I slide my hands up his chest to the thick column of his neck.

"I know you want me," I say. I lean forward and press my lips to his neck. "I want you, too." It's now or never. He hasn't shoved me off his lap yet, so I'm going for it.

I pull his face down and kiss him.

His lips are a firm line for a solid minute, it seems, before he growls at the back of his throat and then devours me. His tongue dives into my mouth. He kisses me hard. It's a claiming and my panties are soaked, my clit is throbbing.

He shoves something on the table behind me, then lifts me onto the surface. His big body looms over me as he pulls my tank top up to my throat. His blue eyes laser in on my bare boobs.

"Wanting you is never the problem. My dick has been hard since the moment I saw you."

I arch my back. "Yes," I whisper.

He palms both my breasts. "Look at how pretty your titties are, angel. So pale and plump." His thumbs scrape across my sensitive tips before he leans down and closes his mouth over one of them.

I thread my fingers through his hair. "Quinn. I want you. Make me yours. Claim me."

He's back to my mouth, kissing me again. He sucks my tongue into his mouth. Then we're making out and it's the very best feeling in the world. The brush of his tightly cropped beard against my cheeks. The sweet taste of the pie on his tongue.

Oh, how I love this man. I want to be his wife and the mother of his children. I don't care how old I am. My granny always said I was an old soul. I know Quinn is my other half. I feel it in my bones.

The sound of his zipper is the most erotic noise I've ever heard and I swear I get a fresh flood of arousal.

And then the doorbell rings.

He stills. Takes his mouth off of me and backs up. His eyes are locked on my body, then he squeezes them shut.

I get a brief glimpse of the significant bulge

behind his boxer briefs before he's tugging up his zipper.

"Cover yourself up." He wipes his mouth, as if he wants to wipe away all memory of my kisses. "This was a mistake." He shakes his head. "I'm sorry, Amber. It won't happen again."

twenty-three

. . .

Quinn

I turn away from Amber because if I don't, I know I won't be able to walk away. Holy fuck. It's been hard enough to stay away from her without knowing how her sweet mouth tastes and how good the velvet hard tips of her tits feel against my tongue.

I adjust my dick as the doorbell rings for the second time. I don't know whether or not to be pissed or thankful for whoever is on the other side of that door.

I swing it open and I'm met with the heated gaze of Eileen Perry.

"Ms. Perry," I say because I'm still not sure if I want to pursue things with this woman. No, I don't want to, but maybe I should. Fuck, the thought of touching her makes me sick though. Not because she's not a perfectly attractive woman. I'm sure she is. But after I met Amber, every other woman might as well be my damn sister.

Eileen clicks her tongue. "None of that. I've told you to call me Eileen." She holds up foil-wrapped container. "I brought you a casserole."

I try to offer her a smile. But I hate casseroles. Truly loathe them. I do not want to eat all my food in a bowl mixed together. I like to know what I'm eating and have each element easily identifiable. Sticking it all in a nine by thirteen dish with some cream of whatever soup and a couple cups of cheese does not make that shit taste good.

Eileen's brows raise.

Then Amber's shoving past me to grab the casserole from the older woman's hands. "Thank you, Ms. Perry. You know how Quinn is, just not much of a talker. I'll put this in the fridge for later."

Eileen's mouth is agape watching my young housekeeper take charge of the situation.

"Come on in, Ms. Perry. I made some pie, if you want a slice," Amber calls from the kitchen.

What is happening right now?

"I don't suppose a bite would hurt," Eileen says. Then she turns and I realize she has her son with her. "Cain, you stay on out here and entertain yourself. Don't wander or get into trouble," she adds with a pointed finger.

Cain. Seems like you're just asking for trouble to name your son after the first murderer on earth.

When Eileen passes by me I nearly choke on the amount of perfume she's wearing. With my eyes watering, I nearly miss her son flip me the bird. Punk. I shut the door. And turn and nearly walk right into Eileen.

"We can sit wherever."

"I set your pie slices on the table," Amber says from the kitchen doorway. "I'm going outside for a bit."

I want to tell her no, that she should stay. But I keep my mouth shut and just walk to the table and sit at the head of the table so Eileen can't sit right next to me.

When she sits I can clearly see that she wears far too much make-up. She'd probably be much prettier without all that caked on her face. The back screen door slams and Eileen jumps in her seat.

"Your property is sure nice out here, Quinn. This ranch is truly beautiful."

"Thank you, ma'am. We do what we can to keep things thriving."

"It's you and your brothers?" she asks. Then she takes a bit of the pie and I want to slap the fork out of her hand. "Whoa, that's so rich. One bite is more than enough for me. Don't want to add anything I can't work off tomorrow morning on the elliptical."

She doesn't even deserve to eat Amber's pie.

twenty-four

. . .

Lone Star
BOSS

Amber

I will not cry.

This is a minor setback, that's all. He doesn't want that woman in there. Or her smelly casserole.

I stomp through the grass and head to the swing that hangs between two large oak trees. It's one of my favorite spots on the property. I'm halfway through mentally reciting granny's recipe for chicken pot pie when a boy appears.

He gives me that look. You know the one. I don't know if boys are just inherently born knowing how to give that look, or if they're taught how to do it at some point. But he's leering at me like he's ready to rock my world.

I roll my eyes.

"Hey baby, whatcha doing out here alone?"

"Trying to get some quiet time. Thus the alone part."

"Don't be like that, we could have some fun while our parental units are doing whatever they're doing inside."

So this is Eileen's spawn. How perfect. "Quinn is *not* my father."

He falls onto the swing next to me and then he becomes some thin armed, pubescent octopus. He's trying to wrap around me or something. One of his hands gropes at my breasts.

"Get your hands off me, you little creep," I yell.

"Come on, baby, I'll make you feel good."

"Yeah, right." I manage to get one of my arms loose and then I'm able to launch it upwards into his face. I knock him straight on the bridge of his nose and I hear the crunch. Feel it too in the way that my knuckles abrade against his skin.

"You damn bitch, you broke my nose," he howls. He's got both hands covering his face now. Blood oozes from between his fingers.

"Maybe that will teach you keep your hands to yourself until you're given permission," I tell him, wrapping my arms around my chest.

"Mommy!" the teenager yells.

There's a commotion at the front door, and then Eileen and Quinn come racing out. As soon as Eileen sees her son's bloody face she screams.

"What happened?"

"That mean lady punched me," he says on a sob.

I roll my eyes again. "Oh please. Your son needs to learn to keep his hands to himself and not just reach over to cop a feel whenever the mood strikes him."

"Well, look at how you're dressed. If that's not teasing him, I don't know what is," Eileen says.

I open and close my mouth several times before I stomp off. Whatever. And Quinn just stood there and did nothing.

> *Me: colossal failure. I dressed like a ho and we kissed.*
> *Me: there was even some first base action & it was amazing.*
> *Birdie: then how did things fail?*
> *Me: saved by the bell*
> *Me: the doorbell. Stupid Eileen showed up with a nasty smelling casserole & Quinn shut things down.*
> *Birdie: I hate that woman*
> *Birdie: maybe he intends to pick things up again after she leaves.*
> *Me: she and her grabby son are gone now. Quinn made it very clear that he & I would not happen.*

> *Birdie: good heavens but the Crawfords are a stubborn lot*
>
> *Birdie: this doesn't have to mean defeat.*
>
> *Me: I don't know what else to do.*
>
> *Birdie: let's think about the books you read.*
>
> *Me: We don't have only the one bed. So we can't snuggle to keep warm, because it's fucking hot outside.*
>
> *Me: It's not Regency England and I haven't sprained my ankle forcing me to live on his couch for a month.*
>
> *Me: We haven't been infected by any kind of bug or disease.*
>
> *Me: neither one of us are in heat and we don't have to procreate to save the world.*
>
> *Me: Should I invent a serial killer or stalker so he has to protect me?*
>
> *Birdie: NO! I've got it! The perfect idea.*
>
> *Birdie: Just get naked and get in his bed. Surely even Quinn can't say no to that.*

twenty-five

. . .

Quinn

It's later than I normally stay awake. I'm a country boy so usually early to rise, early to bed. Tonight I'm being a pussy and piddling around in the barn in hopes that Amber will be asleep when I go inside. And I'm trying to get rid of the restless energy I still have from nearly beating that Eileen's teenage son to a bloody pulp. Thankfully I only grabbed him by the collar and growled menacingly in his face. But I meant what I told him, if he ever touches Amber again, he better hope I call the sheriff because getting in trouble with the law will be a whole lot better than the beat down I'd give him. I don't give a fuck how old he is.

Thankfully, the lights are off and the house is

quiet when I creep inside. I fight the urge to climb the stairs and check on her.

Instead, I pad quietly to my own room. My bathroom light is still on and illuminates a swath of the floor leading to the bed. That's when I realize my bed isn't empty.

Nope, Amber is curled up and sleeping soundly, her arms wrapped around my pillow like she needed to be close to my scent.

Her arms and shoulder are bare, her back too.

I tug on the sheet just enough to confirm to myself that the little minx crawled into my bed completely naked.

I stare at the curve of her hip, then because I can't help myself, I dip my hand into my pants. I squeeze my throbbing cock.

"Goddamn you, angel baby," I groan.

Amber doesn't even stir. I stare at the pale softness of her skin. So flawless and sweet.

She rolls to her back, unfolding herself from the pillow she hugged. Now her fucking titties are just there, bare and on display. And just like that I remember her kiss, remember the way her hard little nipple rolled against my tongue.

My balls tighten. Oh fuck, I'm going come. I pull down my pants to release my angry dick. Then I'm spraying white ropes of come across the sheets and her skin.

She moans and her body arches.

And I turn to go, disgusted with myself for abusing her sweet, sweet body like this.

Twenty minutes later, I'm laying at an odd angle across the old weathered couch in our barn office. And my phone rings.

"What?" I bark.

There's a low chuckle I recognize immediately. "You need more hugs, big brother," Roe says.

"Is there something you wanted?"

"Where are you? You sound like you're in a wind tunnel," Roe says.

I sigh. "I'm in the barn, actually. On Dad's old couch."

"What the hell are you doing out there?"

"Long story."

"The gist?"

"Keeping myself away from Amber."

"Why?" Roe asks.

"She's nineteen years old."

"So? That makes her a legal adult. She's old enough to vote, so our country believes she's capable of making at least that kind of decision."

"I'm twelve years older than her, Roe. She's innocent and sweet and I'm so—"

"Fucking cranky? Yeah, the rest of us had a meeting and we decided it's because you need to get laid."

"Asshole," I mutter, but I feel a grin tugging at my lips.

"Callie tried to put our age difference in between us. I tried to stay away from her because of my felony record. She's a librarian for fuck's sake. We don't match. But, Quinn, hear me when I tell you, that woman lights my soul on fire. She breathes air into my lungs every day. I love all of y'all, my siblings, you're my family. But Callie is my reason for being on this Earth. If you've found that kind of love, then you grab onto it with both hands."

I release a shaky breath. I feel all of those things he described. From the moment I first saw Amber, I felt a stirring in my soul. Like something inside of me was awakening. Every day it grows stronger, louder, more insistent.

So I tell my brother about Eileen's visit and about her punk of a son putting his hands on Amber.

The anger still pumps through my blood like poison. "She broke his nose. Little fucker."

"Amber is a pistol. She fits in our family and none of us think she's too young for you or that you're too old for her."

"You've discussed it?"

"Of course. We talk about you behind your back all the time."

"Well, that's not surprising." I rub my hand against my beard. "That little fucker is closer to Amber's age than I am. Do you know how much I hate that?"

"Because she's yours."

"Damn straight she is. Goddammit, Roe. What if three years from now she changes her mind and she wants to trade me in for a younger model?" Fuck, I sound like a pussy.

"Does that sound like something she'd do?"

"No. Not at all."

"Then there's your answer. Sleep on it tonight, then tell her how you feel tomorrow. When life drops your soulmate in your lap, you don't shove her off into someone else's."

"Since when are you so smart about everything?"

"Prison. I read a lot of books while I was there," he says with a chuckle.

"Thanks, man."

"Anytime."

"So, what was the reason you were calling?"

"I drew the short straw."

"Fuck you," I mutter. "But if that's true, I'm glad. This conversation would have gone a lot differently had it been with Hayes or Johnny."

We hang up and I stare into the darkness for a while. I agree with the sentiments Roe made, but that's all assuming that Amber and I do belong together. How are you supposed to know when you've met your soulmate?

twenty-six

. . .

Quinn

By the time I wake up and finish my essential morning chores, I'm not any more certain about anything than I was the night before.

Do I want Amber? More than I've ever wanted anything or anyone.

Would I treat Amber like a goddamn queen? You're fucking right I would. And I'll love her better and stronger than anyone ever could. Because I do. I love Amber Richie. Everything my brother said last night resonated because I feel it with my angel.

Amber is my soulmate.

My room is empty and my bed is made. I try to ignore the disappointment I feel. It's my own damn fault I left last night. I could have crawled into bed with her. That's what she wanted.

But does she truly know what she's asking for?

I pick up one of the pillows and bring it to my face to breathe in her scent. I bet my sheets are covered in that fruity smell she uses on her body. But her body wash and shampoo are not what I scent on the pillowcase.

No, I smell her arousal. That musky, scent makes me salivate. And I continue sniffing around the pillow like I'm a goddamn blood hound. Right on the edge, where the seam is hidden by the case, I swear to fuck I can smell her orgasm.

My dick goes from semi to raging hard-on so fast, I nearly get lightheaded. I drop the pillow and march upstairs to find her. Enough is enough.

I unfasten my jeans to give my poor dick some breathing room as I reach the second story.

I pause and listen, and I hear it. She's in the shower. I start peeling my clothes off on the way there. She wants to play games, I'll fucking show her who's in charge.

The bathroom door is slightly ajar so I creep in, and she's singing. It's a Carrie Underwood song, if I'm not mistaken. I peer behind the shower curtain to find her rinsing her hair, eyes closed.

I slip inside the shower and grip my cock because holy fuck, she is a vision to behold. Curvy, slick flesh, ripe for the taking.

She opens her eyes, sees me and screams. Her feet slip and she nearly falls, but I grab a hold of her and pull her close to my body.

She swallows. "Morning, Quinn."

"Morning, angel. I've got a question for you."

"It couldn't wait until I was finished with my shower?" she asks.

"Nope. I need to know the answer now."

"Okay."

"Did you rub that sweet pussy of yours on my pillow?"

She gasps and her pupils dilate. "Yes."

"Did you make yourself come?"

Her head nods.

"So you humped my pillow until you came all over it?"

"I did." She bumps up her chin, her gaze defiant and proud. "Maybe I should be sorry, but I'm not. I was sleeping in your bed and I was surrounded by your scent. Then I had a dream that you came in and jerked off all over me, and I woke up and I needed you, Quinn. But you weren't there."

"You've pushed me too far this time, angel. I've tried to keep you at a distance. Tried to keep you safe from me so you could be with a man your own damn age, but I'm done playing the good guy now."

"I don't want a man my age, I want you."

"Get down on your knees," I tell her.

I hold her hand, keeping her steady while she lowers herself.

"You've made me hurt, I'm so fucking hard for you. Now you have to pay the price."

She nods. "I'm sorry I made you hurt. I'll fix it. I promise." She's eye-level with my cock, but her eyes are focused up on my face. It's the hottest thing I've ever seen.

"Put your hands on the backs of my thighs." She obeys. "Good girl. Now, open your lips so I can fuck that sassy mouth of yours."

"Oh God," she whimpers. Again, she does as she's told, parting her lips.

I lean forward and smack her lips gently with my cockhead. She's got me so wound up, it'll be amazing if I don't bust a nut the minute she closes her mouth around me.

"Open up wider." Then I slide my dick against her tongue and I groan. The first feel of her mouth and I have to put one hand on the shower wall. I grab her wet hair with my other hand and pump my hips slowly.

As much as I talk about punishing her, I wouldn't hurt this woman if there was a gun pointed at my head.

Her lips close around my cock and suddenly she's hollowing her cheeks and sucking me hard.

"Angel, goddamn, your mouth feels so good."

She moans around my dick, the vibrations adding yet another sensation.

"Does this turn you on?" I ask.

She nods, her mouth pumping up and down on my sensitive length.

"You like sucking my big dick?"

She bobs her head even faster now and I've lost all control of the situation. "Amber, I'm gonna come," I growl. I try to pull her away with her hair, but she won't budge. "Angel baby, you gonna let me come down your throat? Ah, fuck." I jerk into her mouth once, twice and then my seed shoots into her throat.

When she's swallowed everything, she kisses my stomach and I pull her up to her feet, then swing her up in my arms. "We're not done."

I turn off the faucet, then carry her down the stairs. She's got her sweet face pressed to my throat and nothing in this world has ever felt more right.

twenty-seven

...

Amber

I would take a moment to relish the fact that my heart is soaring if I wasn't so damn horny. But right now I am ready for Quinn to do whatever to me to make this aching between my thighs stop.

I'm so wet it's embarrassing, and I'm not talking from the shower. I've only ever seen a dick when I Googled some stuff after reading a particularly enlightening romance novel. Who knew there were that many sex positions?

Quinn puts me down at the foot of his bed, then stands behind me. His big hands reach up and cup my breasts, pinching my nipples. I lean my head back on his chest, because that's where I reach him. My head hits the middle of his pecs.

So yeah, we have a size difference. And we have an age difference. Still, we somehow fit, like two broken pieces of pottery forged back together.

"Get on the bed on your hands and knees," he says.

I do as he tells me knowing I'm about to be spread out where he can see just how wet I am. The minute I'm in position he groans.

"Angel baby, you're dripping down your thighs."

I shift my body, pushing my ass back towards him.

"You need me to take care of that sweet pussy of yours?" he asks.

"Yes, please."

The bed creaks and jostles as he gets on behind me. "Spread your legs a little wider."

I wonder if I should tell him that I'm a virgin. I'm guessing he's figured that out, but surely he's not planning on my first time being doggy style. Isn't that supposed to be extra deep and intense? I probably should have gone to the library and checked out some actual non-fiction books on sex to figure out more about the mechanics, instead of relying on Birdie's romance novels.

But then I feel his hot breath on the backs of my thighs and a brush of his lips. Oh, is he going to…?

My question is answered a second later when he licks me. Just straight up tongues my pussy like he's making out with it.

"Oh my God. I never read about it like this," I murmur stupidly.

He chuckles against my tender flesh and it lights me up. The sound, the fact that I made him laugh, the vibrations of his breath against my clit.

I lean my head down on the bed because I'm whimpering and feeling like I'm going to collapse at any moment from how good his mouth feels on me.

His tongue swirls around my clit, then presses inside my pussy. I squeeze my eyes shut and fist the sheets. Then I rock back against him, once, twice. I'm essentially fucking his face, and it feels so dirty and so perfect.

Then his tongue is back on my clit and he slides one, then two fingers inside me. His touch reaches a spot inside that I've never felt before and pleasure pulses through.

"Oh, yes, right there. Do it again."

So he does. Over and over.

"I think I'm going to come," I say.

His lips close around my clit and he sucks and that sends me careening over the edge.

"Quinn, Quinn, Quinn," I chant his name as my orgasm charges through me. He licks me until every last wave of pleasure subsides.

Then he rolls my boneless body over so I'm starfished on the bed. He chuckles, then slowly kisses up my body.

When he reaches my face he smiles down at me. "Just what have you been reading?"

"Birdie made me do it."

He laughs again and this time, it's full bodied.

I smile up at him. "You are stupid handsome when you smile."

His brows raise. "Is that a good thing?"

I cup his face. "Yes, but I like your scowls too."

He shifts his body further up and I feel the heavy weight of his erection against my belly. "I want to fuck you raw. I don't want anything between us anymore. Not even a condom. You on the pill, angel?"

I shake my head.

"Do you want me to use a condom? I will if you insist, but I'm claiming this pussy and if that means I put a baby in you, then so be it. This is just the beginning."

"Don't need a condom. I just want you." I pull on his underarms. I spread my thighs wider and raise my legs up. "Fill me up, Quinn. Now. I've been waiting for you for so long."

His intense blue eyes meet mine and I almost say the words. I almost tell him I love him. But I don't know if we're truly on the same page, and I don't want to risk breaking the fragile place we're in.

He reaches between us and glides his cock through my arousal. Watching him do it is so sexy, I gasp. "This is going to hurt, so I'm gonna do it fast, then it'll get better. I promise."

"Okay."

He thrusts inside of me and I feel a sharp pain and then stretching, so much stretching. I wince and he places sweet kisses all over my face.

"It'll never hurt again, angel, I promise. I'm sorry, Amber. I'm so damn sorry."

"It's okay. It isn't really hurting anymore."

He drops his face into the crook of my neck. "Your pussy feels so good. Feels like it belongs to me."

I want to tell him he can have my pussy, my heart, whatever he wants. I'll be his, now and forever. But that's when he starts to move and all I can think about is the slide of his cock inside me and how it hits every nerve. I think he's hitting my G-spot when he presses in and then when he pulls back, he's somehow rubbing against my clit.

"Oh wow. It feels amazing. So good, Quinn." I wrap my arms around his back and my thighs around his waist. Then he picks up speed and pounds into me.

"I need you come on my cock, angel. Think you can do that?" he asks.

"Yeah, I'm getting close. It's so good. I know I already said that."

"That's it; I can feel your pussy getting tighter. Oh fuck, you're getting close. Goddamn, angel, you're gonna strangle my dick."..." He leans up, bracing himself above me so he can look into my face.

A couple more thrusts and the orgasm explodes out from my core. I cry out his name, clawing at his back. He stills and I feel the hot wet spurts of his release inside me. Then he collapses on top of me and kisses my neck and face.

He withdraws from my body and I feel the loss immediately. But he smiles down at me so sweetly. "I'll be right back. Don't move," he tells me.

Then he comes back with a damp cloth and cleans his spend off of me.

"Sleep in here with me," he says. It's not a request or a question.

"If you hold me for a while."

He nods, his resting scowl face back in place. He climbs into the bed behind me and pulls the covers over us.

Then he's the big spoon to my little. I've never felt so safe and loved. I just wish I knew if this was for tonight or forever.

twenty-eight

Quinn

I wake up to Amber's sweet curves pressed to my body. I open my eyes and find her blonde hair spread like a halo on the pillow next to me. My heart thumps strongly, beating out a love song for her. I realize I've never felt more at peace, more certain about my life or my future.

I'm gonna marry this woman. Today. Which means I've got to get out of bed and get things moving. I extricate myself from the covers without disturbing her. Then I pull on some clothes and grab my phone. For what I need to get done today, I'm gonna need my sister's help.

I'm about to call her when I realize she's already standing in the kitchen.

"Christ, Madison, you scared the fuck out of me."

She smirks. "Morning to you too, big brother."

"What are you doing here so early?" I ask. Then I pour myself a cup of coffee, thankful again for the programmable feature on our machine. It's the simple things in life.

"I heard a rumor and I wanted to come talk to you about it before work. Normally you're already out with the cows this time of day."

I grunt and take a sip. "Roe is giving me the morning off. Now that he's finished with this semester, he has time to do more out here."

She nods.

I roll my eyes and sit at the kitchen table.

She comes and sits with me.

"There are so many memories in this room," I murmur.

Madison smiles wistfully. "Yeah. I miss them both."

I swallow thickly around the lump in my throat. "Me, too. I suspect we always will."

"But we'll be making new memories here. Roe and Callie will be starting a family soon, I imagine. Harrison and Birdie probably won't be too far behind them. Now you and Amber." She stares at me over her coffee mug.

I know she's wanting me to acknowledge my feelings for Amber. But all I can think about is that my sweet angel could be pregnant with my baby right now. "I want to marry her," I say.

"No shit."

"Mad, I'm serious."

"So am I. The rest of us have been talking about you for weeks. How you've been stomping around like a giant toddler whose toy is too high for him to reach."

I chuckle. "Whatever."

"What are you going to do about it?"

"Already done. She's in my bed right now."

Madison's face scrunches up. "Gross. I do not need details about my brother's sex life. I meant about the marriage. You have to get a license and then wait three days."

"Three days? What the fuck for?"

"Texas law. I don't know. I own a trinket shop, I'm not a lawyer. Call Blake."

That definitely delays my plans, but doesn't change things too much. "I need a ring."

"She needs a dress."

"Right." I scrub my hand across my hair. "I don't know how to plan a wedding."

"Of course you don't. I'll help. I'm sure Callie will too. And I can probably recruit some friends. I bet Savannah would do her hair and make-up."

"Who?"

"Savannah, from the salon downtown." She waves a hand dismissively. "You probably don't know her because she's younger than me. But you might remember her brother Luca. He's in the FBI now."

"Oh yeah. I would have sworn that Luca and Jackie Garcia would end up together. High school with them was like non-stop verbal foreplay."

Madison's eyebrows go up. "Interesting."

"Speaking of people from high school, did you hear that Wade Guidry is coming home?"

"Yeah. He deserves a fucking parade for losing his leg like that."

"He did receive a Medal of Honor and a Purple Heart."

I nod.

"One thing you might want to do is extinguish the rumors Eileen Perry is spreading about you and her."

"What the hell is she saying?"

"That y'all are going to get married."

"Fuck no!"

"I'm just saying, that's what some people think."

"Well, they're wrong. I wouldn't marry her under any circumstances."

twenty-nine

...

Amber

I got the 9-1-1 text from Callie fifteen minutes ago. I could hear Quinn in the kitchen talking to his sister so I wrote him a quick note, then raced out to Quinn's truck. Ten minutes later, I pull up to Rory's house. It's a ranch-style house, blue with white trim and a great porch that wraps around on one side.

I can hear her animals bleating and whinnying and all the other noises her farm of miniature animals make.

It only takes me a few seconds to find the hidden key where Callie said it would be, and I let myself in.

"Rory," I call. "It's Amber. Callie texted me and said you needed some help."

And then I hear the unmistakable sound of vomiting. Not my favorite, but I took care of granny until she passed and cancer is not kind to the body.

I find poor Rory looking pale and hugging the side of the toilet bowl.

"Oh, sweetie, what can I do to help? Is it food poisoning again? Callie mentioned you had it a while back. Maybe stop eating the grocery story sushi."

She glares at me waving a hand to indicate I should leave.

"Okay. Well, I am going to go to your kitchen and see what I can find for you. Holler if you need me." Once in there I find saltines and an electrolyte drink. So clearly this isn't her first bout with this illness.

"Goddamn Crawfords. How is it even possible for one family to be that attractive? It's stupid," Rory mutters as she comes into her kitchen. She lowers herself to a stool at the breakfast bar. "If the thought of eating didn't make me so sick I'd have a big Crawford boil. I bet the Guidry's could make it nice and tasty." Then she snort laughs. "See what I did there?"

I laugh because even sick, she's still adorable with her ragged red braids and freckled face. "Crawfords—crawfish. Super funny."

She narrows her eyes at me and points a finger in my direction. "You've got a hickey on your neck roughly the size of Rhode Island, I'm guess the eldest Crawford did that to you?"

I self-consciously rub my neck, but can't stop the smile from spreading. "He did."

"They're irresistible, aren't they?"

My stomach knots. "What?"

"The Crawfords. All of them. So attractive. So damn irresistible." Then she looks up at me and gives me a weak smile. "I'm pregnant."

My eyes go wide. "By one of them?"

She wipes at the corners of her mouth, and then nods.

Car doors slam outside and then Quinn and Madison bust inside.

"Angel, I don't know what you think you heard, but I made my sister come so she could clear up any misunderstanding," he says. His thick chest heaves with his labored breathing.

"I don't even know what you're talking about. I got a text from Callie saying that Rory needed help so I took your truck and came right now. I knew y'all were visiting," I motion to him and Madison. "I didn't want to take the time to interrupt. So I just left that note."

"So you didn't overhear anything?" Madison asks.

"No. Why, what did you say?"

"It doesn't even matter now. Come'er." He holds his arms out to me and I don't hesitate.

He hugs me tight.

"I'm gonna be sick," Rory mutters, then she's racing to the bathroom.

"Oh dear, is she okay?" Madison asks.

"She will be. In about nine months," I say.

"No way!" Madison says.

I nod. "And evidently it's one of y'all's. I mean obviously not yours, Madison."

"Can y'all stop talking in girl code?" Quinn asks.

"Rory is pregnant with a Crawford kid," Madison explains.

The siblings look at each other, then march down the hallway to the bathroom.

"Johnny or Hayes?" Quinn demands.

Rory's sitting and leaning against the tub. She looks up at us. "Who do you think? I can't believe I was so stupid."

"Okay, I've got this," Madison says. "You two, clear out. Go home and settle all the things. And I will take care of our little mama here and my niece or nephew she's growing. I'll let you know if I need anything," she adds when I try to speak up. Then she dials her phone and calls some woman named Bonnie and asks her to be in charge of the store that day because she'll be out sick.

I take one more look at Rory and give her a smile. "It'll all be okay. Eventually." Then I glance at Madison. "I'll see if we can't find some candied ginger somewhere in town and bring it by. That might help."

Madison hugs me. "Welcome to the family," she whispers.

My eyes fill with tears. I had somehow forgotten that if I get Quinn, I get an entire family. A big, loud, crazy family that's always in each other's business—I've never had that before. Now, I can't wait.

thirty

. . .

Quinn

We're barely outside of Rory's house when I pick Amber up. She wraps her legs around my waist and I press her to the side of the house and kiss her.

I press our foreheads together.

"I thought you'd left me," I whisper.

"Never, cowboy. I'm so in love with you, you're a part of me now. If I ever left, it would destroy me because you're grafted on my soul now," she says.

I reach into my front pocket as best I can. "We can get you something different if you want. But Madison reminded me, that since I'm the oldest, this was mine to give." I hold up the ring. "This was my mama's ring, I think you would have liked her, and I know she would have loved you."

"Quinn," she whispers. Her beautiful eyes are swimming in tears.

"Marry me, angel baby. Put me out of my goddamn misery so I know you're mine forever and no one else can touch you."

She grabs my face and kisses me. "Yes, I'll marry you. But for the record no one else can touch you either. If that skank Eileen comes sniffing around, I might break her nose this time."

I chuckle. "You came out of nowhere and I wasn't prepared, but you're the best thing that's ever happened to me. I need you to believe that, Amber. I love you, angel. I love you, I love you, I love you."

"Can I have the ring now?"

I slide it on her finger and it fits perfectly. "Are you always going to be this demanding?"

"Probably."

"I'm going to spoil you so good."

"Can we go home and you can do that thing with your tongue again?"

"Gross! Come on, can't a sister eavesdrop on the romance part without hearing about my brothers' sex lives?" Madison yells from where she's pressed against the window next to us.

"Serves you right for being so damn nosy," I yell back. Then I carry my woman to my truck. And we go home and I do that thing with my tongue. Again and again.

epilogue

. . .

Lone Star Boss

Amber

1 year later…

Quinn's got his giant paw across my eyes and he's walking me slowly into the house.

"This is ridiculous, you know. I would have kept my eyes closed."

"I don't know, angel, you can't always be trusted. You've got a naughty streak as long as my arm."

"That means it's almost as long as your—"

"Gross!"

"Stop!"

I'm met with a chorus of yelling Crawfords begging me to stop talking. I swear if I'm about to say something dirty, there's at least one of his siblings around to hear it. I have impeccable timing.

"What?" I ask innocently. "I was just gonna say almost as long as his boot."

"Uh-huh.'

"Sure."

Finally we're inside, the door is closed behind me and my husband removes his giant hand from my face. Everyone is here. All the Crawford siblings and their partners.

"Did you bring it?" Quinn asks Roe who nods in return. Then they meet in the middle of the room and Roe hands Quinn a box.

"What's with all the secretive glances?" I ask.

"I should have done this a long time ago, but better late than never," Quinn says and he holds out the box.

I go to take, but he won't release it.

"You should sit down. On the floor," he says.

"Oooookay." I'm in the middle of lowering myself to the floor, not an easy feat when you're seven months pregnant with a giant's baby. The rest of the Crawfords all start sitting on the floor too. I frown at them. "Y'all are being so weird."

Then Quinn is at my side and he's set the box in front of me. "Now you can open it."

"It's not like a severed head or anything, right?"

"Where the hell would I find a severed head?" he asks.

"Body farm isn't too far from here," Madison says.

"True," Johnny agrees. "Also, there's bound to be some buried out in that big cacti field behind the Jergensons' property."

"Rhetorical question, crazy people," I say. But I'm laughing because I love them all. Even though they're up in our business. We're just as much in theirs. We're one big family unit. Then I hear scratches from inside of the box and I shoot a questioning glance at my husband.

He holds his hands up in innocence.

I peel open the lid and am met with four blinking eyes. Two green and two copper. I reach in and pull out, the smallest, fluffiest, cutest kittens I've ever seen. One black tuxedo, he's the one with the green eyes. The other one is an orange tabby cat.

My eyes fill with tears because I'm fifteen months pregnant with the world's biggest baby. "Are these for me?" I ask, cradling them under my chin.

They mew and cuddle up into me. And my heart melts.

"I know you never had any pets."

"But you said cats belong in the barn where they can kill mice and stuff," I say with a sniff.

"I did say that. But I'm an idiot sometimes. What my angel wants, my angel gets."

"Eventually," Hayes adds.

"Everything is all set up in the laundry room too. Litter boxes and food and water bowls," Madison says.

"What are you gonna name them?" Birdie asks.

I hold up the black and white one. "This is Biscuits." Then I hold up the tabby. "And this is Gravy."

"Now I'm hungry," Johnny murmurs.

"You're always hungry," Roe tells him with an affectionate smack on the back of his head.

"Biscuits and Gravy it is," Quinn says. "All right, who brought the food because my angel baby is growing a human and doesn't need to be cooking for everyone right now."

I laugh, but I stay right where I am, snuggling my new fur babies surrounded by my surrogate sisters and brothers. Life is good.

thank you for reading!

I hope you loved these first three Crawford cowboys. Please consider **leaving me a review**. Want to know who knocked up Rory? You'll find out in **Lone Star Playboy**.

Join my newsletter for bonus epilogues, deleted scenes and a FREE BOOK.

If you liked this cowboy,
you'll love my other cowboy books!

Virgin Cowboy
Curves and Cowboys

See ALL of my books.

Want to connect with me?

> *Join my Facebook VIP reader group: Baxter Babes*
> *Friend me on Facebook*
> *Follow me on Pinterest*
> *Follow me on Instagram*
> *Follow me on Twitter*
> *Follow me on Bookbub*
> *Follow me on Goodreads*
> *Visit my website for excerpts of all my books.*
> *Visit my author page on Amazon for links to all of my books.*

I also love to hear from readers so feel free to drop me a line anytime.

saddle creek, tx: the crawfords

. . .

WELCOME TO SADDLE CREEK, TX. *Cattle ranches scattered amidst the rugged hills; the land dotted with wildflowers, cacti and longhorns. Small town, but home to the big Crawford family. These cowboys and mountain men have been busy working their land and haven't had time for romantic complications. But when the terms of a will mandates they all find brides or risk losing* *their family's land? It'll be a race to the altar as each of them is determined to do their part to save their slice of heaven. But none of them expects that finding a bride will also mean finding love.*

Pre-Order the entire series here

about the author

USA TODAY BESTSELLING AUTHOR, Kat Baxter writes fast-paced, sweet & STEAMY romantic comedies. Readers have dubbed her "The Queen of Adorkable." and her books "laugh-out-loud funny," and "hot enough to melt your kindle." She lives in Texas with her family and a menagerie of animals. Kat is the pseudonym for a bestselling historical romance author.

What readers have said about Kat's books:

"Kat Baxter is my catnip!" ~ Goodreads review

"Whenever I need my sexy nerdy dirty talking romance fix, I know Kat Baxter has my back!" ~Goodreads review

"How does Kat Baxter make me fall in love with her characters in just 12 short chapters? It's coz she's a freaken magic weaver with her words!!" ~ Amazon review

"You'll instantly fall in love." ~Goodreads review

"Swoon. I could not get enough of this story and fell in love with both these characters!" ~Amazon review

"… the chemistry between them is instant and off the charts!" ~Amazon review

"… original, hot, and a hoot!" ~Amazon review

"DAMN it's hot." ~Amazon review

"… sweetness, heat and humor. By the time the story was over, my cheeks hurt from smiling so hard." ~Amazon review

Made in the USA
Columbia, SC
30 May 2023